G R JORDAN

A Rock 'n' Roll Murder

A Highlands and Islands Detective Thriller Book 33

First edition

ISBN: 978-1-915562-87-6

*This book was professionally typeset on Reedsy.
Find out more at reedsy.com*

I'm not God but if I were God, ¾ of
you would be girls, and the rest would
be pizza and beer.

AXEL ROSE

Contents

Foreword

The events of this book, while based around real locations around Scotland, are entirely fictional and all characters do not represent any living or deceased person. All companies are fictitious representations. Only 3 note bar chords were used in this book.

Acknowledgement

To Ken, Jean, Colin, Evelyn, John and Rosemary for your work in bringing this novel to completion, your time and effort is deeply appreciated.

Books by G R Jordan

The Highlands and Islands Detective series (Crime)

1. Water's Edge
2. The Bothy
3. The Horror Weekend
4. The Small Ferry
5. Dead at Third Man
6. The Pirate Club
7. A Personal Agenda
8. A Just Punishment
9. The Numerous Deaths of Santa Claus
10. Our Gated Community
11. The Satchel
12. Culhwch Alpha
13. Fair Market Value
14. The Coach Bomber
15. The Culling at Singing Sands
16. Where Justice Fails
17. The Cortado Club
18. Cleared to Die
19. Man Overboard!
20. Antisocial Behaviour
21. Rogues' Gallery
22. The Death of Macleod - Inferno Book 1

Kirsten Stewart Thrillers (Thriller)

Jac Moonshine Thrillers

1. Jac's Revenge
2. Jac for the People
3. Jac the Pariah

Siobhan Duffy Mysteries

1. A Giant Killing
2. Death of the Witch
3. The Bloodied Hands
4. A Hermit's Death

The Contessa Munroe Mysteries (Cozy Mystery)

1. Corpse Reviver
2. Frostbite
3. Cobra's Fang

The Patrick Smythe Series (Crime)

1. The Disappearance of Russell Hadleigh
2. The Graves of Calgary Bay
3. The Fairy Pools Gathering

Austerley & Kirkgordon Series (Fantasy)

1. Crescendo!
2. The Darkness at Dillingham
3. Dagon's Revenge
4. Ship of Doom

Supernatural and Elder Threat Assessment Agency (SETAA) Series (Fantasy)

1. Scarlett O'Meara: Beastmaster

Island Adventures Series (Cosy Fantasy Adventure)

1. Surface Tensions

Dark Wen Series (Horror Fantasy)

1. The Blasphemous Welcome
2. The Demon's Chalice

Chapter 01

Larry's head ached. He tried to give it a shake, but that made it worse. Deep down, he was sure his brain was loose and floating around within his head. He tried to open his eyes. He tried again. On the second effort, some blurred images seemed to make their way up to his brain. He closed his eyes and tried for a third time. There was such brightness. Where did that come from?

Larry gazed down his body, first looking at his chest, with the beer belly that stuck out from underneath. Beyond that, he could just about see his genitalia, and his toes curled up at the far end of his legs. *What time of the day was it?*

There was no duvet over him. There was no duvet on the bed. But there was someone else on the bed. Larry gazed to his left. There was blonde hair, but it was tangled in a bit of a mess. A youthful face looked at him. She had a lot of make-up on. But it couldn't hide the fact that she was in her teens. Very late teens, hoped Larry.

He pushed himself up off the bed, swung his feet round, and almost collapsed. His head didn't seem to obey what he told it to do. Seemingly, there was an enormous weight at the top of his body, one that, when he leant anywhere, wanted to fall instantly to the ground. This was his room, wasn't it?

Larry gazed around. Yes. There was the wardrobe. It was half open at the moment, and inside was a naked woman. Sitting beside her was powder on the floor. That might have been the expensive stuff. There were plenty of beer bottles around the bedroom, too.

As Larry finally got to his feet and staggered across the bedroom, he spotted a third woman, again, with nothing on. All three women seemed to be out for the count. And the thing was that Larry was struggling to remember any of them. There was a redhead. There was the blonde. And there was the brunette. That was right. Donal had said to him, 'You want to go for the hat trick, Larry? Take them all in.'

Where's Donal? thought Larry.

Donal was one of Scotland's top musicians. Or at least he had been. Back in his day, he was a rock superstar. He still was in a lot of ways. People mentioned him, after all. He could still pull out the old tricks on stage. He could still play a guitar. Although these days, it was mainly festival gigs. And not the proper ones. The ones where he turned up for maybe a twenty- or thirty-minute set. That was about all he could handle.

And the stress of getting him up there was bad enough for Larry. He didn't need to get him into a fit state to perform two or three hours a night. That was back in the day. But back then, they were wild.

Larry looked around him. Actually, the wildness hadn't gone, had it? As he stepped across the room, the redhead girl opened her eyes.

'Where's Donal, sorry—'

Larry couldn't remember her name.

'Fags,' said the girl suddenly. 'Fags, you are F—'

She fell asleep again. Fags, as Larry was known in the industry, shook his head and wandered out of the bedroom into the hallway. Lying in the hallway was another woman. This one was partly dressed, in the sense that she had a Viking hat on, and was holding a plastic sword and a shield in the other arm. Helge? That was her name, wasn't it? Or was that the name she used last night?

Fags looked down at her. He tried to stare at her more closely, intrigued by her body, but as he leaned over, his head slid uncontrollably, or so it seemed. His eyes swam, and he thought he was going to be sick.

What the bloody hell time of day is it? thought Larry. He padded naked along the corridor, and then into the living room, hoping to find Donal in there. But there was no Donal. There were, however, many women, all sleeping in various positions. The air was full of stale sweat. There was also old alcohol in the air.

Larry looked around at several bottles of the good stuff. Although, considering the amount they'd consumed before touching it, he doubted they could remember what the good stuff tasted like. He spotted his gown on a chair on the far side of the lounge. Larry walked over to it, and at the third attempt got it on, tying up the gown before sitting down on the edge of a seat.

On the seat was a blonde-haired woman, snoring her head off. Like the others, she had nothing on. Unlike the others, she seemed too paralytic to be concerned. Maybe I'll get a little shot of something, Larry thought. He looked over to one sideboard in the room, and saw a bit of paper. *That's what the powder had been in*, he thought.

Larry walked over, hoping to snort something up his nose,

but found the powder sachet to be empty. *Had he used it all last night? Was that really it?* Suddenly, he burped. It was a sickly burp, but it woke up one woman opposite him. Maybe, last night, she had looked insanely attractive. At the moment, she looked almost insane.

Her hair was a mess. She seemed to be covered in crisps or some sort of foodstuff. Somebody, at some point, had obviously smeared chocolate all over her. It had now rubbed everywhere. Larry noticed that the carpet was looking distinctly ruined. That probably would have been Donal as well.

'Where's Donal?' asked Larry.

One woman, the blonde, stood up. She walked over to Fags and put her arms around him. He wasn't sure if it was for support or to show affection, or was she just doing what she was paid to do. Her eyes were glazed over.

'I don't know,' said the woman. 'He went away last night. Disappeared. Didn't he? You didn't, Fags. You're my bronco. You're my—'

Larry turned away, pushing the woman backwards. She fell over onto a pile of other bodies. But instead of hauling herself back up, she just lay there. The place was a complete mess, but the cleaner would come in. Sometime. They rarely asked for the cleaner until about three.

If the women were still here, the Russian woman that cleaned used to get annoyed. Well, what did she think had gone on? If you took the women out of here, you'd still know something was up.

Larry walked out to the kitchen and found another woman there. How many had there been? This was Donal, wasn't it? He liked plenty of women. Well, willing women. Hookers,

4

really. Prostitutes. Women that would just say whatever to him. Gratify him. It wasn't what he really liked. What Donal used to like was the groupies. That floated his boat. They would have done whatever for him and all for free because they worshipped him or, at least who he was up on stage.

Larry had never been a musician, but Larry had been good at managing musicians, and picking Donal to manage had been one of the best decisions of his career. At least it had been. The man was a has-been now. Yes, he could play notes, but he couldn't handle the crowds the way he used to. He tried to talk Larry into releasing a new album, and Larry had fought with him over it—until eventually, he relented. That's why they were here, in Donal's house. There was a recording studio attached on to it. Well, a little distance away from it. Maybe he'd gone there. *That would be it*, thought Larry. But he needed to be up and playing soon.

It was one thing that Larry could never fully understand. How Donal could go from a rammy such as this, into the man with the voice of, well, not an angel, but at least something useful on a record? Larry turned to the refrigerator, opened it up, and took out a large bottle of milk. He poured himself some into a glass, which he had lifted out of the cupboard, before leaning backwards onto one of the kitchen benches.

Larry drank the milk, forcing it down. He knew some people would throw an egg in there, but he would not do that. Every time he had a hair of the dog, Larry found he threw it back up again. Not Donal. Donal would have another couple of drinks and then play.

Larry made his way out to the rear of the house to a small swimming pool at the back. There was also a jacuzzi tub and inside he saw two women. The bubbles were going, but both

5

the women looked very bleary-eyed.

'Fags,' said one, 'we woke up in here. We just put it on to keep warm. Is that okay?'

'I need you to be out of here soon, all right? Jump in the shower, get cleaned up. Then lose yourselves, yeah? Donal's got work to do. Have you seen him?'

There was a shake of the head from both of them.

Must be in the recording studio.

Donal did this sometimes. He'd get up at stupid o'clock and just start playing his guitar, totally smashed out of his mind. There was nothing produced that was of any use. Yet Larry had heard him record sometimes. He needed to be half awake at least to produce a melody.

Larry was worried that when he'd come next time, he'd have to bring the band. But these parties would get even more out of hand then. He looked around him and counted another two women outside. The man had too much money, way too much money. Larry looked over at the recording studio, which was blurring. He stumbled over towards it. The wind blew hard against him and he found his dressing gown had opened up at the front, sending a chill exactly where he didn't want a chill.

He pulled the dressing gown closed and walked over to the recording studio. There seemed to be smoke coming out of the top of it. What the heck was that? Slowly, Larry approached. He reached forward to the door handle. His first thought was it felt hot.

Was it a fool's instinct? Was it just something had awoken inside of his brain? Part of him was saying don't open the door. He reached down with his hand, then lifted it off again. That was hot! Or at least he thought it was hot. Was it hot? Surely, it was hot. He wasn't just imagining it.

6

His head ached. Part of him felt like he was going to throw up, but Larry needed to get Donal on the move. He undid his gown, stretching it forward onto the handle, and then opened the door. He quickly let go as the door swung open, wrapping up his gown again. Looking down to focus on tying the gown again, his eye was off the interior as it was revealed. When he looked back up, he was taken by surprise.

The heat inside was intense, but it almost took a while to register with him. He stumbled back a bit, but then Larry stumbled forward. Donal was in here? Why was it so hot? Why was there a fire? What was going on?

As Larry stepped further in, the fire felt stronger. Suddenly, he stopped at the far end of the recording studio. Donal was sitting on a stool. Or was he? Maybe he was propped up on the stool, as opposed to sitting of his own free will. There was a guitar sitting between his legs. It looked more like an album cover than the scene of a rapidly occurring disaster.

He wasn't playing the guitar, for it wasn't across his shoulder. Instead, it was sitting upright, the instrument's neck reaching up past his own neck. Fire was raging inside, as Larry suddenly felt even more hot. He went to stumble forward. But flames were now whipping in from either side. The fire was spreading fast, gathering in ferocity.

Suddenly, Larry stumbled backwards towards the door, put his hand on the wall, yelped with pain, and then turned to look back at Donal. Beside Larry, a naked woman appeared, and she shrieked.

'FIRE!' she cried. 'FIRE! That can't be.'

She turned and fled. Larry turned to look for Donal, but bits of ceiling were falling down in front of him. The carpet was ablaze, sparks were coming off electrical equipment. A hand grabbed him and pulled him outside.

'Get the fire brigade, Fags. We need the fire brigade.' Fags turned to see a red-headed woman. She had been up by the pool, just lying there. He needed the fire brigade; he needed his mobile. He reached for it. No he didn't have it on him, did he? Where the hell was the mobile; what had happened last night; where was it?

Larry stumbled hard, forcing his way back towards the house. Then he shouted out loudly, 'Fire brigade, somebody get the damn fire brigade! It's—Donal. Donal's on fire.'

Chapter 02

Hope was happy. She was sitting on a beach at Chanonry Point with the day just starting. Last night had been terrific, and today she didn't have to work. Instead, she had attended a concert along with John. It had been a while since they'd been out together properly. He had talked about taking her for dinner, but she'd seen the gig in one of Inverness's clubs and convinced John to go along.

Hope enjoyed music, but more than that, she enjoyed the party atmosphere. She loved to jump around in a crowd. At least she had done, back in her slightly younger days. John hadn't really seen that part of her yet, but she'd been all for it last night. Jeans, t-shirt, leather jacket. John had tried to look the part too, but it wasn't so easy. He didn't seem to mind, though. He'd spent most of the evening with his arms wrapped around her, as Hope sang the songs that were blasting from the stage. And then he'd jumped about with her, which had taken her by surprise.

He wasn't dull, but John was quite staid. So, when Hope took off, as one of the raucous songs at the end took hold, she hadn't expected John to leap forward with her. Deep amongst the crowd who were bouncing off each other, she hadn't expected him to pick her up on his shoulders. They had jumped further into the crowd before he got bashed, and the pair of them fell over. She got up to her feet laughing and when they came out of the concert, she saw he had enjoyed his time, too.

He'd gone along for her, not just to keep her company but to share the experience with her. So, she thought she would push for more. They'd headed off to a pub, and he'd had a couple of drinks before she drove them out to Chanonry Point. It was around two in the morning when they got there, wrapped up, her leather jacket around them both. They'd shared the morning together, intimate, and something truly precious.

And now she was sitting, watching the waves roll onto the beach, John's arm around her. He was leaning up against a wall, half dozing, but she was feeling terrific. She'd taken a risk as well because she was on call, which was why she had drunk nothing. True, a call would always be possible, but it had been quiet lately. And she needed this night. They needed it. It had been good and now nothing could break this special moment. She leaned back into John, who wrapped his arms tightly around her. Hope felt his kiss on her neck, and then more. She responded in kind until her phone vibrated.

'Sorry, I've got to check it,' said Hope. 'You know I'm on call.'
'I know,' said John.

Hope looked down at her phone. 'Aw heck, it's Seoras,' she said. She dialled his number, calling him back from the text.

'Rise and shine. Hope I didn't get you out of bed,' said Macleod.

'No, you certainly didn't get me out of bed,' said Hope.

'Good,' said Macleod. 'You ought to head off straight away, then. We've got a—hang on, can I hear the sea?'

'Yep, just having a little early morning walk down by the

beach,' said Hope.

'Right,' said Macleod, clearly not understanding. 'Sorry to bother you, but I need you to get down to Strontian.'

'Strontian? Why? What's down there?'

'The house of one Donal Diamond. Apparently, he's some sort of rock superstar. Never heard of him. Not sure what type of music he plays, but there's been a fire. Uniform are down but they don't like the look of it. We need somebody to get down and just assess what's truly happened. See if we've got a proper investigation on our hands.'

'Of course,' said Hope. 'I'll get down just as soon as I can. I think Perry's in as well, isn't he?'

'I haven't called him yet. Went straight to you,' said Macleod.

'I'll get on my way, then. Donal Diamond, blimey,' said Hope. 'Not surprising though. He was a right rocker back when I was a bit of a wild child.'

'I'm glad somebody knows him,' said Macleod,

'I'll get on my way then.'

'What do you mean, *wild child*?'

'Well, I liked to party quite a bit. Diamond went off the rails whereas me, I was never really off the rails.'

'Get down, do an assessment, tell me what's going on,' said Macleod. 'I'll be in the office most of the day. Got to shift a bit of paperwork. Clarissa wants a meeting as well. Apparently, she wants me to take some sort of arts course.'

'All right. What did you tell her?'

'Told her as soon as she got on a new DI course, I'll get on the arts course,' said Macleod, laughing.

'I'll catch up with you,' said Hope. She closed down the call, leant back, and kissed John. 'Sorry,' she said. 'Gotta go to Strontian.'

'Where's that?'

'South?'

'Will you be away the night?'

'Don't know. Possible murder. Donal Diamond. He's dead.'

'Is that the rock guy?' asked John.

'At least you've heard of him. Macleod didn't have a clue.'

'Not really Macleod's sort of thing, though, is it?' said John.

'No, it isn't. Let's go,' said Hope.

John grabbed her, pulling her back into his embrace. 'No, we need to finish this off properly,' he said. He kissed her deeply, then smiled at her. 'You need to show me more wild times,' he said. 'This whole side of you, I don't really know that well.'

'I used to be quite—Seoras would have said hedonistic. It's a posh word.'

'What's that mean?'

'Sort of Ibiza vibe, but probably there's more of a rock chick in me.'

'Well, I liked the rock chick last night,' said John.

Hope smiled, stood up, and put her hand down for him. 'Come on, let's get going.'

Hope allowed herself a five-minute shower when she got back to the house, but retained her leather jacket as she made the office. She was travelling down to Strontian and as a DI, there was pressure to dress smart. Instead, she put on what she loved, her jeans, her t-shirt—a clean one though—and beamed when she met Perry in the office.

'Time to go,' she said.

'Really?' asked Perry. 'Where are we off?'

'Thought I'd just let you get in and get your breakfast, have a cigarette.'

'Well, that's all done,' said Perry. 'Where are we off?'

'Strontian. Donal Diamond's dead.' She watched Perry raise his head to the air, thinking.

'Rock guy. Played the guitar. Him?'

'Well, so far everyone's better than Seoras.'

'Macleod wouldn't know him,' said Perry. 'You want me to drive?'

'Take my car down. But yes, you can drive. Are you going to need to smoke when you drive?'

'If you don't want me to, I won't smoke. It's your car. Ross doesn't like me smoking in the car.'

'If you have to, you have to,' said Hope. 'But you roll the window down when you do it, OK?'

'I'll try not to,' said Perry. 'But thank you.'

Hope placed a phone call to Ross, advising him of the situation, and telling him to follow her down as soon as he was able. She then placed a call to Jona Nakamura, the forensic lead in the station, but she was already on her way. By the time Perry raced off out of the station, the dawn was fully up and Hope was feeling more relaxed.

'You don't mind if I say something,' said Perry.

'Well, I won't know until you say it,' said Hope. 'Will I?'

'No,' said Perry. 'I hope you don't think I'm forward.'

'I don't mind forward,' said Hope, 'but if it's going to be something inappropriate.'

'I promise it won't be inappropriate. You were out last night, weren't you?'

'Why do you ask?' said Hope?

'Well, at the moment, I think you look like you could do with an hour or two's sleep. You're not your usual one hundred per cent switched on. Don't get me wrong. I'm not saying you're doing anything wrong. But you're not fully loaded.'

13

'Okay,' said Hope. 'And—'

'You can get some kip, if you want. You obviously had a good night.'

'Why?' asked Hope.

'Jeans. T-shirt. New T-shirt. New jeans. I don't think you were wearing those last night. Your hair's brushed. But it's not been washed. You had a shower. But you didn't wash your hair.'

'We'll stop there, Perry, shall we?' said Hope.

'Sorry, I just wanted to ask if you wanted to nod off for a bit. I mean, leave the phone out. If Macleod calls, I'll wake you. After all, there's nothing else to do at the moment, is there, until we get down.'

Hope stared at him. He was quite something, Perry. Macleod had been right. He saw things, picked up on minor details about you. And yes, he was a man's man? Was he from a time that was now really meant to be forgotten? Maybe. He may struggle with being in the modern age, but he'd been polite enough there. And ultimately, he just wanted to let her get some sleep.

'Thanks, Perry,' said Hope, taking out her phone. She left it in front of her, and turned over slightly and soon nodded off.

Perry woke Hope up approximately two minutes before they arrived in Strontian. He looked down at his own phone, checking if he'd had the right address, but then saw the police car across the driveway.

'I don't think you're going to like this. I can see press here already,' said Perry.

'I guess it's to be expected,' said Hope. 'I mean, it's Donal Diamond. We'll get inside into the driveway before we discuss anything.'

Perry drove the car in front of the police car, rolled down the window, and pulled out his warrant card.

'DC Warren Perry. This is DI Hope McGrath. We're here to look into the situation.'

'I'll just move the car and let you through,' said the constable. 'Sarge is up at the house at the moment. It's all a bit chaotic.'

'How do you mean?' asked Perry.

'Fire service is just about done. The fire's out. I believe your forensic team is here. Miss Nakamura. She's looking at that side. We're having to keep everyone away from the bodies in there. We've got a lot of women here. When we arrived, they were all walking around naked. A guy in the middle of them. I believe his name was Larry Goodlad, but everyone seems to call him Fags. They're the only people here.'

'A lot of naked women?' said Hope, leaning past Perry.

'Yes, we're sort of struggling to try to—well, get them all clothed. There's a minibus arriving for them or something.'

'Thank you, Constable,' said Hope. The constable moved the police car and Perry proceeded up the driveway with the car. He parked just short of the main building. As he stepped out, Hope walked round the car to him.

'Can I trust you with these ladies?' asked Hope.

'Of course you can,' said Perry.

'No saucy comment?'

'What do you want me to say?' asked Perry. 'You've made it quite clear that sort of banter wouldn't be appropriate. Okay, so I will not use it. Does it feel like one of the better days at work because I'm about to round up a load of naked women? Well, yeah, probably. But, they've maybe seen somebody die. By the sounds of it, this sounds like a drug and booze party. So, I don't think it's going to be all pleasure.'

'Sort them out,' said Hope. 'Find out where they've come from and what's going on with them. Don't let them leave.'

'Of course not,' said Perry. 'Where do I catch you?'

'I'll see Jona. I think I need to get Ross down here as quickly as possible.'

Hope looked around her. There were several women walking back and forward. Some had blankets around them. Some were wearing odd bits of clothing. Firemen walked here and there. She turned and looked at the press. Cameras snapped like Hope was in the middle of London fashion week.

Yeah, that's what they'll want, thought Hope. *Lots of police and half-naked women walking around. Tabloids will love this.* She turned back to Perry. 'Perry, get the women somewhere less exposed, and get them, well, less exposed.'

'Will do,' said Perry.

He marched up towards a minibus and Hope saw him talking to a man inside it. The man seemed to argue with Perry, but Perry was quite insistent. As she walked over to talk to Jona, she heard him talking to the fire crew, asking for silver blankets, or anything else they had.

Last time out, she hadn't worked with Perry. She'd left him with Ross. Maybe he was just keen to make a good impression by letting her sleep. Maybe he was showing off, telling her what she'd done last night. But when she looked at him, she saw how his eyes were everywhere, taking in every detail.

Well, you can't stand and assess him, she thought. *You best get on with it and go see Jona.'* Hope turned to walk up towards the fire-ravaged building. The smoke was still thick in the air, along with the undeniable smell of human flesh. She took in a deep, sobering breath. John's arms seemed a world away.

Chapter 03

Hope stood examining the site of the recent death of Donal Diamond. There was the small burnt-out recording studio alongside the house where a night of debauchery, drink, drugs, and, obviously, plenty of sex had happened. The place was a constant hive of uniformed police, many of whom Hope had pulled in from the larger areas. Strontian was out of the way, but fortunately Perry seemed to come into his own.

Previously, she thought of him as the thinking-type of guy. It's what Macleod had sold him to her as. A man who would look at things from a different angle. Right now, what she needed was someone to take hold of the situation and start organising the team. Ross had always done that. As a constable, Ross was always the responsible one, picking up all the paperwork, sorting out all the details, even making the coffees.

Perry had seized his opportunity. While Hope was working away on the site, Perry had obtained a small centre in Strontian, and was already getting constables to outfit it for the team. They could be down here for a while, Hope reckoned. She had briefly met with Jona Nakamura, and her team was already inside the burnt-out remains of the recording studio.

Hope was keen to speak more with her, desperate to find out what had happened inside, but she knew better than to harass Jona straight away. Besides, she'd have a fire specialist with her, looking for the source of the fire, how it had spread, and how Donal Diamond had remained trapped.

At first look, suicide was a possibility. The man had enjoyed copious sex, by the sounds of it, however. The women that Perry had been instructed to look after had said briefly that they were having sex with both men who were inside the previous night. Larry Goodlad was the other man, also known as Fags because of the number of cigarettes he smoked.

Larry admitted to having sex with the women—admitted to it all being a wild rollercoaster of a night—at least in the quick interview the constables had completed with him. Hope would speak to him in more detail, but she wanted to get a few bits of information first. Ross would arrive soon, any moment in fact, and she would welcome him. She felt quite stretched now with just herself and Perry. Perry had spoken little to her since he went off to organise everything. Hope was working her way round from constable to constable looking around a house that also was draped in forensic operations.

A car pulled up outside the cordon and Hope saw the rush of the press. They were everywhere outside the grounds, which didn't really help. The roads out around Strontian were okay for the small number of locals, or the odd tourist. But they weren't designed for heavy amounts of traffic. Donal Diamond's death, surrounded by a bevy of naked women and drugs and booze, would be all over the press and each newsperson was there to get their story.

Perry had done well with the women, keeping them away

from the *vultures* as he described them. But the press were there for a reason and they'd have their part to play. For now, she hoped the constables deployed would keep the scene secure.

The car wove its way through the police cordon up onto the driveway and parked up. Ross stepped out, smartly dressed as ever, and almost marched over to Hope.

'What have you got for us?' he asked.

'I'll walk you around. Susan, take the car and go back into Strontian. Perry's got a small centre there. He's got some of the young women who were involved in last night's shenanigans. Help him interview them. He'll bring you up to speed on what's happened. I'll take Ross round here.'

Susan Cunningham nodded, got back in the car and drove off towards Strontian.

'How are we looking?' asked Ross.

'I think we've got most bases covered. Perry's done really well. He's set up a centre in Strontian. We'll be able to work out of there. He's booked some accommodations as well. I think we'll be here at least two or three nights, if not more. I don't really want to leg it back up to Inverness and back down every morning.'

Ross nodded, but his face looked dejected.

'I'll see if I can get you back sooner,' said Hope. 'It's the boy, isn't it?'

'He doesn't like it when I'm away,' said Ross, referring to his son. 'He says Angus is always there, always ready to care for him. Says I run off to look after dead people.'

'But he's not far wrong with that, is he?' said Hope. It was meant as a humorous remark, but Ross didn't seem to take it as such.

'Come on,' said Hope, 'I'll walk you round.'

Hope led Ross over to where Jona's team was working in the recording studio. She stood at the edge and then saw the diminutive Asian woman emerging from the building. She was chatting with a fireman, but she broke off on seeing Hope.

'I've got some big news for you,' said Jona. 'Oh, hi, Ross.'

'Big news,' said Ross. 'What's that?'

'Your rock star didn't kill himself. He was murdered.'

'Murdered?'

'I believe so. Doesn't look like he struggled whenever the fire struck him. If he killed himself, it would have been a poisoning.'

'Poison?' queried Hope.

'Yes. I believe he was poisoned. In which case, why set fire to the place? All seems bizarre. I think he was murdered. I'll have to examine the body, toxicology, all the rest of it. But at the moment, run with that premise. Although I wouldn't announce it to the press.'

'Suspicious death, then,' said Hope. 'Oh, it'll keep them interested, anyway. I'd rather you said it was accidental. We'd have cleared this lot out the front in no time.'

'So, did he start the fire?' Ross asked.

'Doubt it. We're still working through all of that. What we know is he was immobilised.'

'Fags said he saw him in there, according to the constables,' said Hope.

'Probably correct.'

'Shouted at him?'

'That could be right, Hope. And he probably didn't react back. Like I say, he seemed to be immobile when the fire struck him.'

'Fags,' queried Ross.

'Larry "Fags" Goodlad. He was here last night, and seems to be some sort of producer or manager working with Donal Diamond on his new record. He's in a bit of a mess.'

'So, who was here?' Ross asked Hope. She waved Jona on, understanding the woman had more work to do.

'Basically Donal Diamond and Larry Goodlad and then there were a lot of women, quite young women. Perry's got them in Strontian to interview them. That's where Susan is now.'

'Well that was good of Perry, wasn't it?' said Ross, almost snidely.

'Don't. He's been as good as gold. I think he's quite concerned for them.'

'Sure he is,' said Ross. 'What else have we got?'

'Follow me,' said Hope, and walked Ross back into the main house. Inside, the remnants of the previous night were still there. Bottles, small packets in which drugs had been held. Chairs were turned over. There were duvets, blankets lying here, there, and wherever.

'Some stink in here, isn't there?'

'Yes,' said Hope. 'It actually gets past the smell of the studio.'

Ross sniffed the air. 'Quite a heavy night then.' Stale alcohol hit his nose, but also the rank sweat. 'How many women were there?'

'Something like twenty,' said Hope.

'Twenty,' said Ross. 'I know it's not my field, but two guys, twenty women. I mean, really?'

'John says he's got enough to handle in this single woman here,' said Hope. Ross looked at her. 'Sorry,' she said, 'just trying to crack a bit of joke,'

Ross looked around. 'When did the fire start?'

'Jona is still working on that. It was definitely in the morning; everything had seemed fine during the night, well, as much as anybody can remember. Also, there were no reports from neighbours. They are not that close, but some neighbours have reported hearing loud music. None of them report the fire, not until much later, at which point it's already been called in.'

'So, we've got a lot of naked women who I take it have been paid to come.'

'They're not groupies,' said Hope. 'I'm trying to find out exactly who they are and where they are from. There was a large minibus turned up for them to take them away in the morning, but he seems to have scarpered.'

'We'll need to trace that then,' said Ross. 'If they're getting pimped out, we'll need to see if there're any connections.'

'Perry's on it. Come through here.'

Hope led Ross through to an office in the house. There were papers everywhere, across the desk, sideboards, and even in and around the drinks' cabinet.

'Get yourself geared up and then get through these papers— see if anything's of use,' said Hope.

'OK,' said Ross. 'What am I looking for?'

'I don't know,' said Hope. 'My thinking is Donal Diamond's dead, so we've got to look for a grudge, maybe. Look for some financial trouble in case it is suicide. But if it's not, this man's worth money. This isn't the only house he owns.'

'Really?'

'No. So we're going to need to look into that. I want to find out where this estate goes now he's dead. Who's his family? One constable said he's got an estranged wife, or a divorced one, something or the other. So, we'll need to look up that as well. These papers may provide some clues or some lines of

22

enquiry to chase along.

'First things first, we need to build up a picture of the man. If he's been killed, why? Given the amount of money he's worth, inheritance is always a good one. But it might not be the only thing. We've got drugs here. Did he owe somebody money? Did he piss somebody off? I need a picture, Ross, and one that isn't generated by those vultures at the gate. And we need to keep it within the confines of the investigation. I want nothing getting into the press.'

'I'll get on it,' said Ross. There was a shout from outside.

'Detective Inspector, Detective Inspector McGrath.'

It was Perry's voice, so Hope left Ross and walked back outside.

'Perry. I sent Susan down to you. What's the matter?'

'Saw her. It's OK. I briefed her. But I needed to come up and see you.'

'Problems?'

'You could say. One of the women is missing,' said Perry.

'Missing? I thought you took them back to Strontian. How did you lose her from—'

'No,' said Perry quickly. 'She's missing from last night.'

Hope's face dropped. 'Are you sure?'

'One of her friends came to me. She was with Donal last night. She didn't say what happened, but when they went to the bus this morning, when the man turned up, she wasn't there.'

'So where did she go? When did she disappear?'

'I've turned to Jona, to see if we've collected the clothes. We'll take them back to Strontian and get the women to identify their own. I'm also going to get some idea of where she might have run and go look for her.'

'Use Susan. Get Susan to do the manhunt bit. You're also going to want a woman there if you find her.'

'If we find her, and maybe she's seen something,' said Perry, 'maybe didn't run of her own free will, we need to be careful. The other friend, she said that the boss, the one who came in the minibus, he won't be happy with them; says he doesn't like them talking. I'm not sure, but I'm not sure these are just ordinary prostitutes. Not simply women who are for hire, proper working girls. I think these people might be trafficked. None of them seem to be British, well, you know what I mean. They all seem to be European.'

'Then hold them,' said Hope.

'Can we get them put up somewhere?'

'Find somewhere, do what's necessary, but make sure that they're protected as well,' said Hope. 'If the guy from the minibus is worried, he might come and try to break them out. He might use force. Sort that side out, Perry, and get Susan to go looking for the other woman. Get a description to me. Ross and I will work from here.'

'We'll need to get on it, quick,' said Perry. 'Her friend was worried. I believe these are traffickers. They won't bat an eyelid at killing one, to keep their secret safe.'

Hope nodded. 'Then get to it.' She watched Perry disappear and realised that her problems had just got a lot bigger.

Chapter 04

'Hello, Mr Goodlad; my name's Detective Inspector Hope McGrath. This is Detective Sergeant Alan Ross. I know you've already done quick interviews with some of our constables, but we're going to sit down and talk properly now about your friend, Donal Diamond.'

'That was his stage name,' said Larry Goodlad. He was dressed in a scruffy pair of jeans, a t-shirt with an 80s metal band on it, and his hair was unkempt. He smelt of cigarette smoke, and his eyes were bloodshot. It was later on that same day and the effects of the previous night were clearly showing.

'I believe you were some sort of manager or recording editor for Mr Diamond.'

'I worked with Donal for years. It was me who made Donal's sound, basically. We go a long way back. Back to the days when he really was famous.'

'So clearly he was no longer at his peak,' said Hope.

'Donal doesn't need to be at his peak. People loved Donal for being Donal. Well, they did.'

'It was only the two of you up here,' asked Ross. 'Why was that?'

'Because that's the way Donal liked it. He liked his women.

In later years, he liked them a fair bit younger than him. He also liked a lot of booze—some drugs, too.'

'Where'd the drugs come from?' asked Ross.

'Donal had his suppliers. I never asked. I don't particularly partake in them. More for the booze. That being said, I had some last night. It was pretty wild.'

'Where did the women come from?' asked Hope.

'Donal made the contact. They arrived in a minibus. There was some guy today wasn't there trying to pick them up, I think.'

'Donal organised all of this?' asked Ross.

'I haven't got the money Donal's got. Donal's worth a fortune.'

'As I understand it,' said Hope, 'he made most of that money back in the 90s. And he was living off it. He hadn't made that many records over the years.'

'Novelty records. He did bits and pieces here and there, over the last, what, twenty, twenty-five years? Thirty years? Blimey,' said Larry.

'And you've stuck with him all the way through it.'

'I have. I've seen everything, including his breakup from his family.'

'Tell me about that,' said Hope.

'Well, he kind of screwed it up. Evangeline and Donal were tight for a while. I mean, he even stopped sleeping with the groupies around him once he'd gone with her properly. And then, Tee-Tee was born.'

'Tee-Tee?' queried Ross.

'Tara. Tara Turner. Tee-Tee That's his name for her. In fact, that's what everyone called her. But his wife, Evangeline, took Tee-Tee when they split up.'

'And they split up because . . .?' asked Hope.

'Because of stuff like this. He's a bit of a sex addict, I guess. I mean, he was. Sorry. He was the archetype rock and roll person. He was the guy who did it all, the guy who ruined his life, the guy who lived his life, I guess, too.'

'Why is he in Strontian?' asked Ross. "Seems a bit of a strange place for the rock and roll lifestyle.'

'Because Tee-Tee's here. Tee-Tee and Evangeline moved here to get away from him. He bought the massive house and built a recording studio.'

'Do you live here with him?' asked Ross.

"No, no, I'm here because we're recording. He's looking to make a comeback album.'

'And how's that going?' asked Hope. 'Or rather, how was it going?'

'His voice is not what it used to be. I mean, we'd have stuck it out, we'd have made money off it. I'd have got decent musicians around him.'

'So take me back to last night,' said Hope. 'You said the girls arrived. What time was that?'

'Blimey, mid-afternoon. We'd done some recording, late morning, and, then Donal says he's not up for it anymore. It's time to party.'

'And so, the girls just pitch up and—'

'The girls pitch up and we're in the pool. I mean, anybody walking in would have got a shock. Nothing on, and yeah, just basically doing whatever we please. Plenty of drink, plenty of drugs.'

'Any of the girls in particular hang around Mr Diamond.'

'No, it's not like that. Donal's, well, he wouldn't really go for someone in particular. Donal's much more of an open-minded

27

pleasure taker. He likes quantity, he likes to, well, try different things with them. I guess most of them would have been with him at some point.'

Hope tried to picture this in her mind. She remembered her nights out with John, and frankly, she thought they were enough for each other. Try as she might, she couldn't imagine all these people, even back in the wilder days of her youth. She wasn't like this. This was just crazy.

'When was the last time you saw Donal?'

'I can't rightly remember. He says to me, 'Fags,' that's my name; he calls me Fags—he's always called me Fags. That's because of the smoking, not because I toadied along to him or anything, at a public school. No, no, no, he calls me Fags.

'I remember I was, I think, in the living room—actually I was pretty chilled out. I fell asleep, and then I woke up and, well, I went through the house, you know, because I wasn't, quite right with it. Not quite sure what was going on. I stumbled around; I was looking for Donal, and I couldn't find him. So eventually, I stumbled out, past the pool, and there were girls everywhere. But he wasn't with any of them, which was unusual.

'And that's when I got to the recording studio, because I thought, well, he might go there. Donal's not completely shallow. He likes his women and his booze and that. He likes all the stuff that would make him out to be shallow. All the stuff all the tabloids love. But actually, musically, he loves his guitars. He loves all that sort of thing. And to find him in the studio just playing or strumming away wouldn't be surprising, even after all of this. He's got a constitution like an ox. He can get up and play after the wildest of nights.'

'And when you got there?' asked Ross.

'I saw some sort of smoke coming out. Not in vast quantities, but when I got the door open, which took time, because it was hot, the place was on fire. Forgive me,' said Fags. There were tears beginning to run down his eyes.

'You see, he was just sat there with his guitar. The surrounding fire, it was intense, really intense. I mean, I could barely stand up. I was in a mess. If I'd been sober, could I have got him? I don't really know. But I was beaten back by the fire, and there was some girl with me, too. But neither of us had anything really on. I had a gown. She had nothing. Ran off and phoned the police, phoned the fire brigade. By the time we got back, well, the place was up in smoke. Everything was a mess, and quite frankly, yeah, it wasn't good. He was gone.'

'Any idea why the place was on fire?'

'No idea. He was a man who was prone to melancholy though,' said Fags. 'I mean it's terrible to take your own life like that.'

'Was the album going all right?' asked Hope. 'Was he keen on it?'

'I think so. Tee-Tee had been over not that long ago as well. He lived for Tee-Tee, really did. Strange he would have left her.'

'Tee-Tee get on well with him?' asked Ross.

'Yes, he did, Sergeant. He deeply loved her but he was struggling to understand her. Maybe all dads are like that. I don't know, I'm not married. Never had kids.'

'What about Evangeline? How did she feel about him?' asked Hope.

'Well, once she got out of the way, I think things were better. Then he moved here. She was worried about his influence on Tee-Tee. She didn't want Tara turning out the same way. Did she hate him? Well, she hated his screwing around that started back up a few years into their marriage. She hated his lifestyle. But she loved him in her own way as well, I think.'

'Is there anybody else you can think of who would wish any harm to him?'

'No one I'm aware of, no.'

'We're not sure it is suicide,' said Hope. 'We're keeping an open mind about his death. Is there anyone from the record industry who would have it in for him? Anyone such as producers, record companies he's worked, with? Has he annoyed anyone over the past years?'

'Oh, he's annoyed plenty of people,' said Larry. 'But there's a difference between annoying them and actually earning them a lot of money. If you annoy them and you're not earning them money, well, they won't tolerate you. But they tolerate, or at least tolerated, Donal, because Donal was a cash cow. The money was always coming in. Donal could afford a lot of things, but Donal didn't know what he wanted.'

'What about the press? I mean, this lifestyle, all of this, it must have annoyed the executives. You don't want to get tainted with that sort of thing, do you?' said Ross.

'Actually, the opposite. That's Donal. Very much so. They wanted it to be like that. They wanted him to be wild. It's the image. It's sold records. They wouldn't care if you had a hotel room wrecked. Easily cover that with the money he was making. And in some ways, Donal was quite easy for them because he kept producing material. Even in these in-between years, he'd try to fudge together a Christmas record or something. Keep bringing himself back up to the limelight, to some degree or other. Donal was a record company's dream. And while he was wild, most of the wildness was contained.

It wasn't done in the high street. He didn't go around playing with kids or stuff like that. No, it was clean, respectable debauchery, I guess. That's probably how they saw it.'

'Did they expect you to keep an eye on him?'

'Well, I always did. Not sure if it was expected or not.'

'I guess Donal was your ticket, as well.'

'I worked with more than him to make my money. I wasn't dependent on Donal.'

'Did you ever get jealous?' asked Ross.

'What do you mean?'

'Well, he had all the fame, all these groupies; he had all the money. You never get jealous of that? After all, I'm sure you put a lot of talented work into making him what he was.'

'Donal looked after me well enough. I made my money but I wouldn't want that hassle. I mean, look at his life. It's a mess. Can't keep a woman.'

'Can I ask your marital status?' said Hope.

'I've never really had the time. I've been quite happy on my own.'

'And currently you're living where?' asked Hope.

'I've got a flat in Glasgow. Mainly work out of there, but I travel a lot with the business. Recording for here, there, and wherever.'

'Where have you been recently then? The last sort of three months, four months?' asked Hope.

'Here, really? Working on this album.'

'OK,' said Hope. 'Don't go anywhere we can't find you.'

'I'll probably stay here.'

'That will not work, will it?' said Hope. 'Best if you talk to Ross here. Maybe get your things on the move. Get you into accommodation somewhere. That would be best. Let us know if you head back up to Glasgow.'

'I will do.' Larry looked down at his feet.

'Are you okay, Mr Goodlad?'

'Yes, Inspector. It's just quite a shock. And I think I'm coming down off a lot of the highs. I think I need to go get some rest.'

Hope nodded, and Ross escorted Larry out. When he came back into the room, Hope looked over at him. 'What do you make of him, then?'

'Talks a good game. Possibly setting it up for the suicide, though.'

'Would you,' Hope asked, 'just go along with this sort of debauchery if it really wasn't your thing? Just, you know, to make up the numbers. The drink, the drugs.'

'No, of course not,' said Ross.

'Well, he's only the first one we've interviewed, but, hmm, I don't know,' said Hope. 'We need to get hold of this girl that's disappeared, and find out about these women. This all doesn't look good.'

Chapter 05

Perry had so many faces to watch he felt he was going cross-eyed. He also felt very sorry for the women who were standing before him. He had gathered them all in the centre in Strontian. It had been used for holding minor events and was afforded a small kitchen at the rear.

Within the centre, Perry had obtained a couple of small rooms to work as offices for Hope and the rest of the team. But the main hall, which was next to the kitchen, he had used for the women who had been rounded up at the home of Donal Diamond. It had been awkward. They'd been wrapped up in silver blankets, most of them not having any clothes because they were in the middle of a crime scene. Perry had organised with a local charity to obtain clothes from their shop. Having got all the women clothed, he had taken down names and established quick interviews.

That was how he knew that there was one missing. Now he was getting the women fed and medically checked over. He was worried that something had been done to them—they may have been drugged—so he brought in a small medical team to advise.

Names were awkward though. Some women didn't seem

to speak English. They were European and there was an occasional smattering of French, but Bulgarian was also spoken. Other languages were there that Perry didn't recognise, and he was having to pull in translators. His deep suspicion was that many of these women had been trafficked. And yet, from talking to his boss, he knew also that Donal Diamond might have been murdered.

But why would any of these women murder someone, then place them inside a recording studio and set fire to it? Something was wrong. At the moment, Perry saw these women as victims, used, taken away from where they were from. Most of them spoke very little, and clearly, they were afraid. The one who spoke the most was worried for her friend. He was waiting for an update from Cunningham on that.

Perry didn't bother to wait and instead dialled Cunningham's number.

'Yeah, Perry, what's up? Kind of busy.'

'You get anywhere?'

'Anywhere? No. I'm being surrounded by these press vultures. Everywhere you go, they turn up. If the woman's got any sense, she'll have run off by the time we get there. I haven't found sight nor sound of her.'

'Keep looking,' said Perry. 'It's important. I think she might hold the key.'

'Why?' asked Susan.

'It's just a feeling. Why would you run off? Why not stay with the pack? And if you run off because you're making a bid for freedom, if indeed it's a trafficked woman, why wouldn't she go to some place of authority? Why wouldn't you hand yourself in, say I'm being trafficked?'

'She might be afraid she's going to get deported,' said Susan.

'Maybe. I think they've been about together for a while. You don't look out for each other until you've had a shared experience,' said Perry. 'That would make sense. I'm just not convinced that they're telling me everything. I'm thinking far from it.'

'Well, you can't blame them, can you?' said Cunningham.

'I'm thinking I might ask the boss if we can put them up, keep them secure, until we can identify if they're trafficked. Or maybe contact the trafficking division. See if they know any of them.'

'That's an idea, Perry, but I've got to get back. Manpower's not great here. I'm trying to get more, but so far, we're coming up against dead ends. On the bright side, we haven't found a body.'

'That is good news,' said Perry. 'Okay, I'll speak to you soon.'

Perry put the phone down and looked at the surrounding women. Some were finishing the meal he'd had gotten for them. He stood up in front of them, trying to cajole them into sitting in a circle. On his side were three different translators. They'd driven in specially when asked and he looked at them, wondering just how this next instalment of his investigation would go.

'I need to ask them all if they know anybody else in this group? Now they might be reticent to say, but I need to get an idea of who knows who. If they don't give names, that's all right. Ask them, do they know the face? Have they known them for a while? See what answers you can get. Don't push them,' said Perry. 'Let them think this is just routine. Take it easy with them. They're frightened. And who wouldn't be? After all, they were standing around starkers in a place where a man was killed. So, easy on it.'

Perry had written the number of questions for the translators to ask each of the women, and he passed these out to them now. He watched as they turned and began working their way round each of the women. He looked across at the two constables also in the room, guarding the doors. Perry wasn't comfortable that the man who had dropped the women off in the minibus wouldn't come back to pick them up. It must have been a large minibus, he thought, almost a bus if you take twenty people. Perry sat behind a desk, sipping on coffee while his translators went to work. They came back to him almost forty minutes later.

'So, we got names?'

'First names on some of them,' said one of his translators. 'They're not keen to give full names. I'm not sure if they're even their real names.'

'That's okay,' said Perry. 'Let's look at some way of identifying them. We can find out who they are later. So, sit down and tell me the answers.'

Perry pulled out a large sheet of paper in front of him. He wrote in a circle each of the names given to him by the translators. He then took out a different coloured pen and began drawing lines across from each of the women who seemed to know each other.

'A few of them have told me about a girl that's not here.'

'Yeah, there's one missing,' said Perry. 'My colleague's out looking for her at the moment.'

'We haven't got a name for her.'

'I'll just put M.G. down for Missing Girl,' said Perry. He noticed all lines were being drawn towards her. She'd obviously been in the group for a while. By the time Perry had finished, everyone had crossed reference to someone else.

Every member of the group was identified as being known by somebody else. Everyone didn't know everyone, but most of the women seemed to know at least ten.

Perry picked up his mobile phone and placed a call to Hope. It rang for a while before she answered.

'What is it, Perry?'

'I've got the women here to go through who they know in the group. This is a pretty, well not tight-knit group, but a group that's been together. Most of the women know at least ten other women in the group. It doesn't look like they've been pulled together from different groups, but they may have been together wherever they were staying.'

'It's an awful big number of women to work together,' said Hope.

'These are trafficked women, Hope,' said Perry. 'I'm convinced of it. I can't prove it, but I'm convinced of it. I don't want to let them go.'

'We can't prove they've done anything. We can't really hold them either.'

'If we let them go, they'll disappear out this door, and the guy will come up in his minibus and disappear off with them. Now, I could track him and follow him, but to be honest, they'll just ship off in the night, head who knows how far away. Dump them off at a house, move them again. We could lose track of them so easily. For their own safety, I think we should put them up in our care. Obviously, we can't put them in our custody.'

'Have you spoken to them about it?' asked Hope.

'Not yet. I wanted your take on it. I don't want to promise things to people when I can't deliver.'

'No, that's wise. Find somewhere we can put them. Make

sure it's somewhere all together. And make sure it's nearby in case we need them. Tell them it's a short-term measure. A couple of days.'

'Can I tell them I'll put a couple of constables with them? Somebody to watch over them.'

'Absolutely. But they also don't go off walking on their own. They stay secluded. They stay away from the press as well.'

'Yeah, that's understood,' said Perry. 'Sounds wise. I'll see what I can do with them. It's not easy. I've got three translators here on the payroll as well.'

'Well, Macleod will have to deal with the budget issue. Besides, I don't think the budget is going to be a problem. Donal Diamond's big news.'

'Well, thank goodness for that,' said Perry. 'At least they're killing well-known people now.' He gave a slight laugh before hanging up and turned to look back at the group of women sitting down on chairs in a circle. He turned to his three translators by his desk.

'Right, I'm going to find them somewhere to stay. I want you to tell them we're concerned for their safety. We would be happy to put them up, feed them, and get them clothed for the next couple of days until we can resolve the matter. They'll not be allowed to go out and about, and they'll have to stay wherever we put them. But they'll have some police for protection. See how they react to that, please,' said Perry. 'I'll just be outside. I need a cigarette.'

Perry walked off for what was only his third cigarette of the day. He could feel the craving. Standing outside of the centre, he could see the minor road that passed through Strontian. It was a small village, very small. And yet, at the moment, there seemed to be so many cars about. The press were also all over the place.

Then he saw himself being watched. He wondered if he would be on the news tonight, smoking a cigarette. Would he be the poster boy? He laughed. No, they'd put Hope up for that, wouldn't they? Hope or Susan Cunningham, but more probably Hope. The DI.

She was good, though, felt Perry. And she hadn't gone on at him. It hadn't gone well when he'd misread the ground. Thought he was joining more of an old boy's network. But with Ross not being that sort of person, he'd had to change his tune. Still, they weren't a bad group to work with. Cunningham was certainly pleasant on the eye, and pleasant to work with and talk to. She seemed to be more normal to Perry. He'd heard of her reputation and thought that was undeserved.

As Perry threw his cigarette on the ground and stamped it out, he noticed a minibus driving away, far down the road. He'd seen it at the house. *So, they are lurking*, thought Perry. They are lurking for the women. Well, he would let nobody like that come and talk to them. If he could get the women sorted and clear, he might try to track down that minibus, see what was going on.

Something was bothering him about Donal Diamond. More than that, about the missing girl. The women he was looking at seemed to be normal. They weren't typical working girls. They were ordinary, as if they'd been dragged away. Most of them were young. Maybe he wasn't sure if they were too young. Maybe they were. He'd find out at some point. None of them gave up their age. Maybe they were told not to do that. Maybe they were young.

He'd have to get some female chaperones. He had some uniformed constables, but he wanted a few big guys around as well who could handle themselves. It wouldn't surprise him if whoever was pimping these women came looking for them.

Perry went to light another cigarette and put it away. Maybe it was Hope. Maybe it was Ross harping on about the cigarettes he had back at the station. Or possibly he just wanted to get these women somewhere safe. Perry walked back inside the centre and spoke again to his translators.

'They all seemed to be amenable. Almost grateful,' said one translator.

'Good,' said Perry. He went on to the computer to look for places where he could put them. He came across a set of holiday homes which were not opening for another two weeks. They looked good and as if they had little access to them, one road into the plot of land they were sitting on. Perry picked up his phone and called the owner.

Ten minutes later, he'd arranged for the holiday homes to be used for the women and stood smiling at them.

'Tell them this,' said Perry, 'that we're off in about half an hour, or as soon as I can get a bus. We're going to take them to a holiday home. We'll stay there for a couple of days at least, and we'll keep them safe.'

He looked at the smiles, as the translators told the women, and Perry felt good about himself, but he also would need to get the trust of the women to learn more about them. He picked up the phone; it was time to call the human slavery division, find out if these women were known. His work would be cut out over the next few days. He felt that although these women had been used by Donal Diamond, they may also be the eyes and ears that the case needed to find out who had killed the man.

Chapter 06

Hope rolled up in the car at the centre in Strontian which Perry had acquired. She stepped out and showed her warrant card to the constable positioned on the door. He gave a nod, stepping aside and holding the door open for her. Ross followed her through. She walked into a corridor to see another police constable positioned at a set of double doors into a hall.

'Constable, I'm DI McGrath. I'm looking for DC Perry.'

'He's just through there,' said the constable, pointing over to another door. 'These rooms down the side are the offices he secured for you. Behind me are the women who were at the house. We've been told to secure them in here. They'll be on the move soon. But DC Perry hasn't advised us where they're going.'

'Good. That all sounds sensible. Ross, with me,' said Hope.

She marched up and pushed open the door that the constable pointed to. Inside, she saw a couple of basic desks with laptops on them. Perry was sitting behind one with a coffee. There was a kettle in the far corner with coffee, tea bags, and milk. There was even a white board on a set of flimsy legs.

'You've been busy,' said Hope.

'I have. Is everyone here?' asked Perry.

'Waiting on Jona.'

'Well, I'll let you get settled in,' said Perry. 'I'll just step out for the moment. Give you the room.'

'You don't have to do that,' said Hope. 'It's Ross and me. Susan's still got to come.'

'I wasn't doing it as a favour to you,' said Perry. 'Need a fag.'

Ross rolled his eyes, but Perry ignored him and marched out of the room, leaving Hope and Ross together.

'Leave it,' said Hope. 'Don't have a go at him. It's just the way he is. I'd hate to be addicted to them.'

'Landed on his feet with this one, though, didn't he?'

'No, he didn't,' said Hope. 'Look, he didn't get off on the best foot with you. Or with me. But he's coming into the team completely cold. He's clever. He's very clever, Ross. In a way that you and I are not. And he hasn't been inappropriate here. In fact, he's been great.'

'Let's hope he stays that way.'

'What is it with you lately?' asked Hope suddenly. 'Alan, ever since you've gone up to Sergeant, you've been proper gripey. What is it?'

'It's nothing,' said Ross suddenly. 'Look, it's—'

'It's because Macleod's not here, isn't it?' said Hope. 'That's what it is, Alan, isn't it? Ultimately, it's the fact Macleod's not here. You liked it when the team was the way it was. You could run around looking after Macleod. Run here and get him his coffee. He appreciated you and he loved what you did on the computers. Now instead, you've got to look after people. And not the uniform constables who are just delighted to step up. You've got to look after whoever.'

'I'll be honest,' said Ross, 'it has been a change. Clarissa is out of the way as well and taking Patterson. It's left us—'

'It hasn't left us as anything,' said Hope. 'This happens. Teams move on. You know? We were with the boss for so long. I'm in charge now. He's still there. He's still—'

'But he's not, is he? Not in that way. He's up above. He's popping down, and he's giving you brief lessons about—'

'Are you not enjoying being a sergeant or something?' asked Hope.

'It's fine,' said Ross, turning away.

'Well, if it's fine, you're doing a poor job of showing it. Because you don't look fine.'

'We didn't pick Perry.'

'And we didn't pick Clarissa either. And my goodness, Clarissa put my back up. She's not me. She doesn't work the way I work. But you know what? Do you know what, Alan? We got through. We managed. Despite the fact the two of us were on the same level. And she had to take a hit too, giving way to me. She had to be *not in charge*. And now she is. Now she's got her own group. It always changes. Maybe you should have gone with her, Alan.'

Ross shot a look over. 'Well,' said Hope. 'We've got a case to deal with. We get on with it. Okay? And if you're looking for the insights from the boss, look to Perry.'

Ross opened up his laptop and sat down behind it. *He was always more comfortable there,* thought Hope. *That's his terrain, the laptop.*

Five minutes later, Perry came back in and sat down. Hope could hear him making a call to the Human Slavery Division, passing on various names. He was trying to get photos to them, to see if the women had been trafficked.

It wasn't long before Jona arrived, clutching several files.

She walked in and looked around.

'Do I sit anywhere in particular?'

'What did you imagine for this, Perry?' asked Hope. 'Where do we brief and discuss?'

'Next room,' said Perry.

'You didn't think you could mention that to us,' said Ross.

'Give it a break, Alan,' spat Hope. 'All right. Well done, Perry. Show me, would you?'

Perry stood up, marched over to the door, opened it, and showed Hope inside. Several tables had been stuck together. It wasn't a perfect round table, but it would suffice. Perry had found another whiteboard and the pens to go with it.

'You've done well,' said Hope. 'Don't bother with Alan. I'll just have a—'

'I'll take care of it,' said Perry. 'He's my boss. I appreciate it, what you're looking to do, but sometimes you have to manage them.'

'Don't do it with such a smile, Perry. You've got until Cunningham gets here. She shouldn't be long.'

Hope watched Perry enter the original office, asking Jona to go through before closing the door. She wanted to push it open and listen to what Perry was going to say. But she didn't. She turned away. They were both big boys. They could deal with it.

Susan Cunningham arrived two minutes later and was shown into the room by Perry. She then held the door open for Ross to join them. All five were soon sitting around the table.

'Okay,' said Hope, 'let's start off with what happened to our man, Donal Diamond. Rock star, ageing, but still worth an absolute fortune. Died possibly in a fire, in his recording studio at his home. This followed a night of debauchery with approximately twenty women, drugs and booze, and one Larry "Fags" Goodlad. What can you tell us, Jona?' asked Hope.

'Well, I'll tell you right now, the fire didn't kill him. Initial tests make us think it was cyanide poisoning.'

'Cyanide,' said Perry. 'That's quite something. Was it self-administered?'

'Not one hundred per cent sure, but if it was my money, this would be more akin to a professional hit, rather than a suicide effort, or something more random.'

'So,' said Hope, 'somebody then set him up inside the recording studio and set fire to it. But why?'

'Something against his music, something against the way he lived,' mused Perry. 'Maybe to cover up, they tried to show it was suicide.'

'Very rough way of showing suicide, though,' said Jona.

'Not if you wanted to get away, Jona,' said Perry. 'Maybe it was an attempt to make everyone think it was suicide while they got out of there. Professional hit. Maybe they just want to put distance between the killing and themselves, and then disappear. Professional people aren't going to be around afterwards. They just need to clear the country. Much harder to go after them after it's all over.'

'It's a good point, Perry. But why is he suffering a professional hit?' asked Hope.

'He's worth a fortune,' said Ross. 'I've looked into the bank accounts. I think we need to look at the inheritance.'

'Well on that, front—' said Hope, but was interrupted by Jona.

'Just before you start, we're looking into the drugs around the house, and the alcohol, tying it in with the idea of Donal being murdered. I'm wondering if the rest of them were knocked out, put to sleep. Somebody would have to drag him or lift him, and put him into that recording studio. Either that or he's gone in there with someone. We're still trying to work out what happened to him.'

'Well, we've got nothing on that,' said Perry. 'These women are not speaking.'

'I take it we haven't got an account of what happened,' said Hope.

'When you say an account of what happened,' said Perry, 'you're asking for places and positions, basically almost like a sex log.' He nearly burst out laughing. 'I don't think they're going to tell you that and how reliable it is when they're all half stoned, anyway. I couldn't say.'

'We still have one missing though, don't we?' said Hope.

'Yes,' said Cunningham.

'Going back to the idea of inheritance. I believe he has an estranged partner or wife. She's called Evangeline Turner. She lives with Tara Turner, or Tee-Tee, Donal's child. I'm going to have to talk to them, see if that's an angle to look at.'

'There are also the guys that brought the women in. Maybe they have something to do with it,' said Perry. 'I think we may need to find them and talk to them. These are trafficked women, so the people that do it wouldn't be averse to trying to dig out some of that money. Is the account secure?'

'Yes,' said Ross, 'there are no unusual transactions coming in and out, no sizeable sums of money.'

Perry nodded, but he looked extremely thoughtful.

'Let's find out where the fortune goes,' says Hope, 'now that we know it's murder. I have had no conversations with the press, but does anybody know anything about anything else in his life? Donal was apparently quite into women.'

'According to the groupies that have been appearing in the locale,' said Perry, ' he was an ever-ready volunteer to their whims.'

'Larry Goodlad said he was very promiscuous,' said Ross.

'They would all have a claim then, wouldn't they?' said Perry. 'How many of them are there?'

'I don't know exactly,' said Ross, 'but we'd have to check through them all, anyway. The press will tell you he's had a child with so-and-so and this person and that person. They've not gone through with the research. They're just reporting hearsay. This is not investigative journalism. This is music news, sensationalism. It's not there to pull refined items out of the fire. It's just tittle-tattle that people like to read. If it's a half-truth, it'll work for them. And even if it's a load of nonsense, it still works for them.'

'In that case, Ross,' said Hope, 'you find out for me what is real. I want to know if he's got children who can inherit.'

'If you don't mind,' said Perry, 'this case is going to be solved if we find our runaway. All the women in there knew each other, and they knew this person. Many of them have said she's not here. If she's run, she's run for a reason. If she's run to get away from traffickers, why hasn't she shown her face to the authorities? Plenty of us walking about. Susan's had plenty of constables scouring the area. Nothing to stop her running out, grabbing hold of one and saying, take me into the station. I need to talk to you.'

'But maybe she's got a fear of being deported,' said Susan.

'What's your biggest fear? The people? Or the country you're going back to? At least you get to tell your story. They don't get to do anything if these are women being trafficked. Think about it; they'll probably be abused,' said Perry. 'This is no life. She's going to want to get clear unless she's seen something else, unless she fears something more. Something is making her hide away from them, from us, from everyone. We need to find what went on in there. These women aren't talking. I need to work on that, but we also need to find our runaway, Susan.'

'Soon as I'm finished here, I'm back out on it. I have teams coming from everywhere, mountain rescue, coastguard search. Pulling in everyone I can,' said Susan.

'Good,' said Hope. 'I'm going to put a call in to the boss. Tell him what we've found. Keep these women locked up tight,' Hope said to Perry. 'I think your idea of keeping them away from everybody and putting a guard around them is good. Make sure that guard isn't too obvious. I don't want the press camped outside.'

'I was going to move them on a bus,' he said. 'Instead, I'm going to move them in unmarked cars and quietly.'

'As you see fit,' said Hope. 'Just get it done.'

The meeting broke up, Jona racing back to the scene. Perry disappeared off and Ross was left behind in the room with Hope as Susan Cunningham went back out on her search.

'I believe he had a word with you,' said Hope.

'He did,' said Ross. 'He actually apologised for his behaviour when he first met me.'

'Good,' said Hope. 'I hope you've apologised for yours in the last two hours.'

'It's not easy,' said Ross. 'You know, when you take the sergeant position, you can do the exams and that, but suddenly I'm meant to just have the role nailed. I'm meant to look after these people. Perry and Cunningham—they've become as thick as thieves.'

'Cunningham and Perry have got something in common. Everyone thought Cunningham was a tart who slept around with everyone. Perry is meant to be some sort of pervert, high on any woman. With neither of them is that the case. That's the slur. So, they bond together. And they're at the bottom. You're no longer at the bottom, so you can't bond the same. You can't be the generous person running around being helpful to all the seniors. What you need to be is my sergeant, driving the investigation, giving me ideas. But you can start off by going and talking to the press. Give them a statement. Nothing exciting.'

'Aren't they going to want you to do that?' I mean, since you are the DI.'

'If there's proper news, I'll tell them. It's a holding statement. So put it together, and put it out there, Ross.'

Hope turned and went to walk back to the office next door. As she went through the door, she stopped and turned back. 'Alan, understand that Macleod told you to move up the ranks. He wouldn't have done it if he didn't think you were capable. For what it's worth, I think you're more than capable as well. But you've got to get over whatever's bugging you, because it's not helpful. You're better than this. Be better!'

Chapter 07

Susan Cunningham was feeling frustrated. There was no sign of the girl. She was also worried. Although it wasn't quite winter, and more like spring heading towards summer, the nights weren't that warm. The girl would go to ground. But where would she stay warm?

Susan had taken a different tack, not being part of the search function. She had tasked, or rather she had requested the help of one of the local search advisors. And although she checked in with him, she wasn't part of the search herself. The teams were searching around different parts of farmland, different places, alongside lochs and rivers, but so far they'd come up with nothing positive. They'd be looking for somewhere a person could crash and bed down for the night.

Susan was worried about the men who had brought the women to the area and how they'd been hanging about, driving the minibus that had been seen by Perry. She stuck her head together with Perry over the phone, and Susan asked some of the local police if they'd seen them recently. When she did so, she came across a young police constable who reported seeing the men.

'They've been about for a couple of days. I don't know

what they've been doing, and I have seen no women with them. When I saw them, they've been driving about in that big vehicle.'

'Like a twenty-person minibus,' said Susan.

'Yeah, I saw it. I didn't wonder where it was going as it was before the murder. The guy who was driving it, he didn't look—well, he didn't look local. I mean we're not that strange a bunch up here, but he definitely didn't give off the impression of being from here. He was more urban.'

Susan wasn't quite sure what that meant. 'How do you mean?' she asked.

'Well, sort of big city-like. A lot of jangly chains and things hanging off him. We just—you don't dress like that around here. I mean, we've got some strange people, don't get me wrong, but not dressing like them. Shoes are too smart as well. I saw them when he stepped out of the bus once. People up here, they like their boots. They like to have things you can walk across rough terrain in. They're wearing big jumpers and coats. This guy's not. He's suited for being somewhere where you're going to be inside a lot of the time.'

'Have you got a description of the people you've seen?'

Susan spent the next hour taking down a description and chatting through with the constable about any further details. Having got them, she checked in with Perry to find he'd installed the women in their temporary abode. Security precautions were set up but Perry was taking himself out of the situation for the night. Susan met up with him and together they did a tour of the local pubs. At each one, Susan spoke to the landlord or landlady asking if they had a large twenty-person minibus parked outside. Or indeed if they had served anyone unusual.

'Well,' said the third landlord they'd spoken to, 'I'm not sure, but my wife may have.' He disappeared into the back of the pub called the Scottish Prince, and a woman with red hair, standing almost six feet tall, came out. Susan was reminded of Hope, except for the fact that this woman had piercing eyes.

'Who are you?' she asked. Susan produced a warrant card, and Perry followed suit.

'DC Susan Cunningham; this is DC Warren Perry. We're up investigating the rather sudden demise of Donal Diamond.'

'Oh that? It'll be quieter about now, won't it?'

'We're interested to know if you've had anybody strange around here lately. Any unusual customers?'

'Well, you've got the tourists coming through, but it's maybe still a touch early. Had some Germans and that. Also, we had, well, there's a group of guys who have come in several times. Four men. Not from here.'

'Where are they from?' asked Susan.

'Big city, I think. They haven't told me very much about themselves. They're buying meals and they're buying drinks, so I don't get overexcited.'

Susan reeled off some descriptions given to her by the constable.

'It could be them,' said the landlady. 'Thing is, when they first came in, they were quite celebratory. They were up for it. Several pints that night, had their meals. They were laughing and joking. They were in—when was it—actually, they were in earlier tonight. You missed them. They were quiet, though. Every night before, they've been really excited. Now they were really quiet. Had their meals quickly. I don't think they actually drunk that much. Other nights they've been on the lager. Always lager. Tonight, coffees, cokes. Bit strange though, you know.'

'You got CCTV outside?' asked Susan.

'No. Not out here,' said the landlady. 'It's not worth it where we are. You don't get any trouble.'

Seems there's been enough trouble recently, thought Susan to herself. *Pity.* She turned and walked out of the establishment, along with Perry, and they stood thoughtfully in the car park.

'Ten o'clock,' said Perry, 'they'll be back.'

'You think? I'm not so sure.'

'No, think about it,' said Perry. 'They've come in. They had a quick meal, Coke's, and gone out. I think they're looking for her. She's missing and they've gone out looking. They've had to come back and have something to eat. But they get too late at night, she's going to have bedded down. They will not drive around in the dark looking for her. It's going to be suspicious. Especially as we know, they've got a minibus. I mean, they've turned up on the scene. They'll be cagey, not wanting to show their hand. They're going to be very worried about us fingering them, making out that they're traffickers.'

'You think they're struggling for money, then?'

'Maybe they haven't got paid yet. Maybe they're still looking to get paid by Donal. Do they know he's dead? Well, the papers will report it. Maybe they'll be looking for the money from someone else.'

'I thought Hope told everyone from her case notes that the women were hired by Donal.'

'That makes little sense, does it?' said Perry. 'He would be dead. You will not get any money from him. The girls are being held by the police. You'd get the hell out of there. Maybe they're still expecting money.'

'Maybe the women know things about them.'

'Either way, they'll be back tonight.'

'I'm still not following you,' said Susan.

'They're off out looking. It's going to get dark. They're going to stop because they don't want to be looking around places in the unnatural hours. They'll attract our attention. Look at these guys: "Oh, what are you doing here, at one or two in the morning?" They'll go to bed, but they'll come back for a drink, because they've come every night for a drink except tonight. They'll come for their alcohol. Trust me. I can feel that.'

'Why? Why wouldn't you just skip it for tonight?'

'Because they're worried. These people are drinkers. Most of the people that traffic are like that. Imagine your conscience. Imagine always being worried about people spotting you, especially at the moment. I mean, things are not going right. They'll be back for their drink. That switch off, that time to enjoy the spoils, so to speak.'

'Okay,' said Susan. 'Ten o'clock now, eh? The pub shuts at eleven. I'll sit in the car with you.'

'Could do with a fag, though,' said Perry.

'As long as you smoke it out the window.'

'Okay,' said Perry. Susan manoeuvred the car to the far end of the car park, where they were sheltered under some trees. It had gone dark anyway, but the car was hard to pick out with no headlights on. Perry had the window wound down and was calmly smoking as they sat together.

'You see Ross,' said Perry; 'how long have you known him?'

'Longer than you, but that's about it,' said Cunningham. 'I've not been on the team that long either.'

'What do you make of him?'

'Good on the computers. Very systematic though. Likes things to be done properly, nice and neat.'

'I must be hell for him,' said Perry.

Cunningham laughed. 'You must be. He's not long up to sergeant. And he's not like Hope. Not like Clarissa.'

'He's certainly not like Clarissa,' said Perry. 'She's something else. I like her though. I mean as a woman, as a person, you know. Don't mean I like her physically.'

'You don't have to explain that to me,' said Susan.

'Well, you know, she's not like you. You've got the looks, you know. I don't mean that as a come-on,' said Perry suddenly.

'You don't have to tread on eggshells round me,' said Susan. 'I'm okay. Say it the way you say it. If you offend me, I'll tell you back to your face.'

'Okay then. Well, you know, you look good. I'm not into Clarissa like that. She's too old for me in that sense, but I like her as a person. She's fun, and she's determined, and she doesn't take no nonsense. Hope doesn't either. I mean, she's another good-looking woman, but she's also, well, I can see why Ross would work better with her than me.'

'She worked with Macleod, though. Macleod's more like you, but I wish I was more like him. His mind is something else, but that's where you and I go together well. I've got the looks,' said Susan. 'I've also got that sprightliness and fighting ability. What have you got? Brains,' said Susan. 'You've got brains. A ton of them. Hope will warm to that. Because you're not just dogged. I'm very like her,' said Susan. 'She needs more people like you. She can do the dogged bit.'

The two sat in the silence, Susan enjoying Perry's company. As they sat, a minibus pulled into the car park, and four men got out. Perry smiled at Susan.

'You want to get the camera?' he said. 'You can get the shots when they come back out.'

They hid in some trees at the side of the car park and Cunningham photographed the four men as they came back out. As the minibus disappeared out of the car park just after eleven, Cunningham followed them with Perry until they arrived at a local caravan site. Susan stopped the car a little distance away, but Perry, watching through binoculars, advised that they were heading into a caravan.

The caravan light stayed on until round about half-past eleven at night, then everything was dark. Perry and Susan made their way back to the rented accommodation the team was staying in. The following morning at seven o'clock, Perry was on his mobile, contacting the owner of the caravan site. He met Susan for breakfast half an hour later.

Susan smiled at Perry because she realised he had something to tell her. His face was almost giddy.

'What's up?' she asked.

'Well, I phoned this morning down to that caravan site. Those guys have got two spare caravans rented besides their own. The owner told me their names, so I'll get that run through human slavery and elsewhere today. Let's see if we know who they are. Apparently, quite a lot of women were in those caravans. The owner said seven, but I reckon they stuck them all in, just didn't tell the owner.'

'So, what, two caravans for ten women each?'

'Sounds like traffic, doesn't it? Sounds like, well,' said Perry, 'it's not good.' He looked up as Ross walked into the breakfast room.

'Do you mind if I sit with you?' said Ross.

'Of course not, boss. Grab a seat.' Ross sat down and noticed Susan smiling.

'What's the biz?' He asked.

'Perry and I found the gentlemen who were driving the minibus about which delivered the women. Perry's got some names. They're on a campsite near to here. Rented out several caravans. The women stayed there one night.'

'I'll put the names through today, see who we can find,' said Perry. 'See if we recognise who they are, but of course, they might be fictitious names.'

'Yeah, they might be. Probably will be,' said Ross. He turned and smiled at Perry. 'It's good, though. Well done.'

'How are you getting on with all the illegitimate children of Donal Diamond though?' asked Susan.

Ross shook his head. 'Rumour, conjecture, innuendo. I deal with birth certificates. I deal with death registers. All the good stuff that tells you exactly what's been reported and you can then cross-reference. You go through the papers to cross-reference rumour and scandal and you end up doubling back on yourself so many times. It's not fun.'

'Not to worry,' said Perry. 'Get some breakfast down you. I'm sure you'll crack it.'

'Will do,' said Ross. 'Will do. And good work, Perry,' said Ross. He stood up and went over to get some cornflakes.

Susan smiled at Perry. 'See? You're making an impression.'

'I know. I had to damn well apologise to him yesterday. Don't know what the guy's so put out about.'

'Me, neither. But I think you're just the person to get it in the neck. I think there's something more beyond it,' said Susan. 'But I don't know if we'll find out.'

'I will,' said Perry. 'I will.'

Chapter 08

Hope had slept fitfully, anxious about the case. She thought it was probably the press attention. After all, it was going to be a national story. Donal Diamond burnt alive in his recording studio, surrounded by naked women, drink, and drugs. It would be a scandal. But she couldn't get caught up in that.

She had spoken to Macleod the previous night, and he had reminded her of that. It was strange having Seoras working this new role, almost grandfatherly. Offering advice, not telling her what to do. It was her investigation, after all. That's what he kept saying. Her investigation. Once she got past the feeling that he was not merely training her, not taking charge of his own investigation—that it was actually her investigation to run—she felt more like a real DI.

Well, until the next time she'd have an argument with him. He had stepped up. He wasn't encouraging his team, pulling the best out of them; instead, he was cross-examining her almost in the way he would be by those even higher above, or by the press.

As Hope parked the car, she stepped out and suddenly found several microphones thrust in her face.

'Detective Inspector, is it true that Donal Diamond has a multitude of illegitimate children, all now laying claim on his estate?'

'I don't work for the lawyers,' said Hope. 'If claims have been made, then maybe you should talk to them. I'm currently investigating his death.'

'Wouldn't such an inheritance make a great motive for murdering Donal?'

'I will not speculate on the reasons for Mr Diamond's death. And I'm also not going to speculate on who did it. I'm running an investigation. Not a murder mystery party.'

It had just slipped out and it probably wasn't a good line to give. Hope wouldn't have given them that when Macleod used to send her off to do the media for him. Where did that come from? Maybe a bit of frustration.

'If you forgive me, I'll have to get to work,' said Hope. She turned and marched towards the building housing her temporary office. As she did, she saw a constable on the door. She stopped and whispered quietly to him.

'How are those people all over my car? Why am I getting a microphone stuck in my face?'

'Would you like a perimeter, Detective Inspector?'

'I'd like the media kept well back from this building. So yes, set up a better perimeter.'

'Will do. It's hard to maintain it, if I am honest, Inspector. We've got so many people off helping the search.'

'Helping DC Cunningham,' said Hope. 'Of course. Okay. Well, do what you can. I don't appreciate getting jumped by the media every time I get out of my car.'

'Yes, Inspector.'

'Just Hope,' said Hope.

'Gavin.'

'Well, Gavin, do what you can. Is anyone inside?'

'DC Ross is already here.'

Hope gave her thanks and then entered the building, finding Ross sitting behind his makeshift desk.

'Do you know what, Ross?' said Hope. 'I've just got jumped by the media.'

'They didn't jump me.'

'No? Well, you haven't had your face in front of the camera too often. I might have to get you to do more of these briefings.'

'I did one for you. It was short. It was succinct. When I drove in today, they didn't say a word to me.'

No, thought Hope to herself, *you're not the tall female.* You're not the one who looks good on the telly.

She remembered in her earlier days being delighted if she was asked to be in a photograph, being asked to front something. Nowadays, it was different. She prided herself on being a detective, being a proper policewoman. Hope wanted to make her mark because of who she was, not how she looked. She knew Macleod valued her because of her abilities. He'd seen past the veneer and saw the heart of who she was. That's why she enjoyed working with him.

There were still others in the force who would look at her the way they looked at Cunningham at times. Clarissa had that over her. Nobody looked at Clarissa for how she dressed or about some fantasy where they would have her on their arm. They looked at her with fear, thought Hope. Then she realised she was thinking too much. Ross was staring at her.

'We're off to see Evangeline Turner,' she said suddenly. 'I want to just discover how many children he's got who may look for an inheritance. She might give clarity about that.'

'Well, it's going to be a lot of clarity. I hope she's got a notebook,' said Ross.

'Why?' asked Hope.

'Well, I've done a bit of work on my last count. I've got almost sixty who have made claims at some point or other about being or having his child.'

'What?' said Hope.

'Sixty,' said Ross.

'You're having a laugh. I'm not pulling in sixty people from around the world.'

'That'd be what we have to do,' said Ross. 'To be thorough.'

'We'll go see Evangeline Turner first. See, if she's in the will as well.'

'She is estranged,' said Ross. 'I gathered that.'

'Well, grab your stuff. You got an address for her?'

'It's down the road from Donal's house,' said Ross.

'Good. Not far then. Car in five minutes.'

When Hope stepped outside, she realised that Gavin had been good to his word, and the press were back out onto the street. The car park was clear. Hope gave them a smile as she saw the photographs being taken of her from a distance. She settled down letting Ross drive her car down to the house.

'Does that not annoy you?' said Ross. 'It would annoy me.'

'It's just one of those things. If you've got looks, people are going to look. If you've got fire, people are going to be drawn to you.'

'It's one reason I don't want my sexuality to be out there,' said Ross.

'I think it's out there,' said Hope. Ross looked across, almost annoyed. 'Well, everyone on the force knows. I mean, even Perry knows now. The press will know. I'm sorry to say that,

61

these days, being gay isn't what it used to be. It's not a big deal anymore, Ross.'

He turned and looked at her as he drove, and then stared back at the road. *He's not sure,* she thought, *if that's a good or a bad thing. I don't know either.*

The car pulled up at a rather posh-looking house, approximately a quarter of a mile from Donal Diamond's. It was probably built within the last ten years. And as Hope looked at it, she thought this was the house that she would have had ten years ago. Nowadays, she wasn't so sure, because she'd want kids now. Didn't she? Did she?

This was the problem. John and she were getting on so well, part of her wanted to settle down. She'd risen to the DI job, but she would not go to DCI any time soon. Maybe she'd want kids.

'Here we are,' said Ross. Hope was aware she was daydreaming again. 'Thank you, Alan,' she said, opened the car door and strode towards the front door. Ross tagged in behind her.

After she pressed the doorbell, the door was answered by a rather tall woman. *She is good looking, though,* Hope thought. *A bit older now, but in her day, she really would have been quite the looker.* She could understand why Donal was her partner. Given his hunger for the female form, she certainly would have taken him by storm. Hope wondered what they had beyond that, though.

'I'm looking for Evangeline Turner,' said Hope.

'That's me,' the woman said quietly.

'I'm Detective Inspector Hope McGrath. This is DS Alan Ross.' Hope pulled out her warrant card. Ross did likewise. 'We'd like to speak to you about the unfortunate demise of your estranged husband.'

'Of course. Come in.'

The woman led them through to a rather grand-looking living room. Large windows allowed the light in from all sides. The settee was modern with crisp corners and bright colours. It wouldn't be something that would be a part of Hope's house in the future. Hope looked around at the various pictures and could see various images of the same girl.

'I take it you are well aware of the passing of your estranged husband?'

'I am indeed,' said Evangeline, a hand running through her blonde hair. 'Fags called me yesterday. It was good of him. Poor man was quite cut up.'

'Was it a surprise?' asked Hope.

'Not at all. Donal was always like this. Debauchery was the reason, really, I left him. I mean, how do you feel as a woman if, all the time, he simply brings in other women? It's one thing if a man occasionally looks at another woman. Even if it hadn't been the odd affair in life, I probably could have handled that. He got a lot of attention. Even when he was truly famous, the groupies would wait for him, offering themselves to him. Now if he had have fallen for one or two of them, fine, but it was a procession, all the time. I confronted him about it and, well, he wasn't going to change, so I left.'

'You didn't leave for a while, though,' said Ross. He had clearly done his homework. 'You were with him for ten years.'

'That's true, but for the first seven of those, it was me. I'm a big girl. I can look after myself. He was screwing around. I was spending his money.'

'And what changed?' asked Hope.

'She came into her life,' said Evangeline, pointing at the picture of a baby on the wall. The child had a giggling look.

Not so many babies sported such a wonderful photo, Hope thought.

'Tee-Tee came into our lives, and Tee-Tee needed a more stable upbringing. You see, the thing was, when I lived in the house, I would come home, and—can you imagine this?' said Evangeline suddenly. She stood up, turning away as she spoke. 'You walk in, with your shopping or whatever, and there, lying across the couch in the living room, is some naked teen. And, if he's been too pissed to move, there's Donal, lying, with all his bits on show. It's not what you want your child coming home to. I could have put up with it for the money, but I wasn't going to have a child see that. And I told him. I said it had to change. But he didn't listen. He didn't want to change. So, I left.'

'How do you support yourself?' asked Hope.

'I'm not in his will, if that's what you're thinking,' said Evangeline. 'I had an agreement with Donal signed. Money coming to me and initially coming to Tee-Tee, so I could look after her. It paid for this. I am well established and have enough money for the rest of my life. I moved to Strontian to get away from the big city and where he would be. He then moved to a quarter of a mile down the road. But I told him then, you come here, you come here on your own. Tee-Tee goes to visit you, you better not have anyone in there. She's got older though, and she knows the truth.'

Hope could hear footsteps on what sounded like a wooden staircase, and a young woman appeared in a leather jacket with long, black hair.

'And this is Tee-Tee,' said Evangeline. 'Once my baby, now my disgusted teen. Have you got any kids?'

Ross nodded, but Hope shook her head. 'Well, just beware,

they're nice when they're young; when they become a teen, oh my goodness—life changes.'

'Stop that,' said the girl suddenly.

'I'm sorry for your loss,' said Hope to the girl. She simply nodded. It wasn't a cold response, but neither was it warm.

'My mum's probably telling you how bad my father was.'

'Well, was he?' asked Hope.

'My father was an addict,' said Tee-Tee. 'Addicted to drink, addicted to drugs, and addicted to sex.'

'When was the last time you saw him?' asked Alan.

'The day he died. I went round that morning, mid-morning, towards the afternoon. Unfortunately, the women were already there. Things were already underway.'

'Blimey,' said Alan. 'That's an early start.'

'That's when I left to do the normal things. Anyway, I'm heading out.'

'Just be on the end of the phone,' said Evangeline.

'Okay,' said Tee-Tee. The girl moseyed out the front door.

Evangeline shook her head. 'That's the way it is now. She was in a foul mood though when she came back. I mean, she defends him now, but she came back from seeing her father that day and she was in a shocker. It was strange, though. She was harping on about the women. See, Tee-Tee's well aware of what he was like.'

'Where did she go the rest of that day?' asked Hope.

'Well, she came back and then had to head out for a therapy session. Same time every week. It's with Mrs Dunstan.'

'Right. What's she need therapy for?' asked Ross.

Evangeline turned and raised an eyebrow at him. 'Her father shags women happily in front of her when she turns up at his house. He's on drink and drugs and estranged from her mother. He followed us all the way out here to Strontian. She gets followed by the press every now and again because of his crazy lifestyle and money. And friends just want to hang with her because they know she's got money. I can't think for a moment why she needs therapy at all.'

Evangeline marched across the living room and poured herself a drink. She turned round, holding a tumbler of whisky in her hand. 'I see why you're the DI and he's the DS. Not the sharpest mind.'

'Well, just to clarify,' Hope said. 'You get nothing from the inheritance money.'

'No, nothing at all. At least, that's what I agreed with Donal. After all, I haven't seen the will. I haven't asked. I'm happy. No idea if Tee-Tee's in it. But I agreed I wouldn't be in it. I would get money up front and I wouldn't be pestered.'

'How did he feel about Tee-Tee?'

'Donal was an arsehole. Loved his daughter, yet he did not know how to deal with it. No idea what to do with her, what to do for her and still maintained this other lifestyle that would alienate her as much as possible. Like I say, he was an arsehole.'

'Don't disappear anywhere without telling us,' said Hope.

'I'm going nowhere. I've had the press come to the door already and I'm not talking to them. If you need to talk to me again, feel free to come back. I'd rather not go to you,' said Evangeline.

'Okay,' said Hope. 'I thank you for your time. I'm sorry for your loss, however you particularly feel about it.'

Hope left the room, followed by Ross as they got back in the car. She knew more and more that she would need to look at these other potential children. Money seemed the prime motive here. She'd have to find a reason beyond it all.

Chapter 09

Susan Cunningham was exhausted. She was checking in with the search party on what was now the end of the second day of searching. Nothing had been found, no trace, no evidence. So, the girl was hiding herself well or someone had already got to her. There were concerns for her safety from the minibus men. But Susan had been watching them, along with Perry's help. She had left him now to cover the night shift, which was decent of him because she was struggling to stay awake.

She had joined Hope for a brief meeting updating her, while Hope provided some information from Jona. It was now confirmed that cyanide poisoning was the cause of death. Jona had got the body back into a proper work room and, having examined it further, she was more and more convinced that this was a professional hit. However, she was keen not to rule anything out until she completed her investigations.

Susan hit her bed sometime around half-past eleven. The place they were staying in was a nice enough house and she didn't hear anybody else arrive. Then the phone beside her bed vibrated in the early hours of the morning. Picking it up, she looked and saw a text message from Perry.

One man gone out.

They were on the move. She picked the phone up and called him.

'Good morning,' he said.

'What the heck time is it?'

'Half-past three. It's a delightful time of the day. One of our minibus drivers is on the move. He headed out, but by the time I went to follow him, he was coming back.'

'Where'd he go?'

'He was away for approximately twenty minutes before coming back. I couldn't get on to him quick enough. It's quite hard following somebody in the dark.'

'And is he back there now?'

'Yes, he is, Susan. But the lights are all still on in the house. He seems to have raised the other three. I think they're about to get on the move.'

'I'll get down there and I'll bring my car,' she said. 'That way, we'll have two cars. I'll stop a distance away, so I can pick them up on the road when they leave.'

'Good,' said Perry. 'I'll let you know when they're departing.'

Susan jumped out of bed, threw off the t-shirt she was wearing, and quickly changed into her underwear. She then stepped into her jeans, boots, and a warm jumper before leaving the house. By the time she'd got in the car, Perry had texted to say she needed to hurry. As she was driving along the road, she had her phone on the hands-free clip in front of her and another text message came through from Perry:

Minibus on the move, headed out towards lodgings. You might pass them.

There was another three minutes before the minibus passed her, going the other way. Approximately ten seconds later,

Perry's car passed her, and he gave her a wave. She turned her car around following in behind him.

It was only ten minutes before Perry texted to say the minibus had pulled in towards a chapel. He said he would stop a little way up beyond it. Susan was only a minute behind him and saw Perry's car heading off the road. She pulled her own car in further up and then walked back to meet him.

'They've gone into the chapel over there,' he whispered. 'I don't know why. I think we need to find out.'

'That chapel's been searched,' she said. 'Nothing was found. We went round all the buildings in the local area.'

'Have you re-searched yet though?'

'We haven't gone back. Not ready to do that. We might look at it again tomorrow.'

'Maybe our lady of the night is cleverer than you think.'

'Lady of the night? What era are you from, Perry?'

'It's a nicer term than saying hooker,' he said. 'I think these women have been forced to do what they're doing. Really changes how you look at them.'

'So, what are they doing here, then? Have they come for her, or have they got something else in there?' asked Susan. 'Maybe they supplied the drugs.'

'You've had people go through here? Yes? How much do you know? Did they search?' asked Perry.

'It would have been a thorough search. After all, they're looking for a person.'

'Exactly. They're not looking for drugs and contraband. So yes, they could be looking after their drugs, but I just don't know. I'm not convinced of the story from Fags that Donal set up everything. Did he look like a guy who could set everything up? You know?'

'What do you mean?'

'How many musicians do you know?' asked Perry. 'I mean successful ones. Ones at the very top.'

'Well, no one. It's not my sort of field.'

'Well, you might be surprised to know that I actually know a few people in that type of business. The ones who are really, really, good musicians. They do a lot of the business inside themselves. They're in charge of it, controlling it. But they're very switched-on people. They're not wild children. People like Donal, they have people looking after them. He's worth a fortune. People make money off him. The record companies will look after him. Send somebody to be there. Somebody that's around all the time. Somebody—'

'Like Fags.'

'Exactly.'

'But you're telling me that Fags was just there to look after him? I mean, he partakes in it all, doesn't he?'

'Yes, he does, Susan, but imagine it. He's told to look after him. Donal will not let him just sit there and watch. He's going to have to get close to him. Maybe he likes the sex and that as well. Maybe he likes the drugs. But he's going to be looked after. He will not be the one sourcing it all, I don't think. Unless the company want him to. Unless they're worried about Donal. But companies rarely like excess of drink and drugs, especially if it stops you playing.'

'So they're OK with the sex, are they?' asked Susan.

'I guess so. I guess it's less likely to stop you playing a guitar.'

'You're giving me a rather poor view of this industry.'

'Oh, there's some very smart people in it, and some who are just dedicated musicians. Donal may be a bit of a dying breed, but he's a dying breed that's still worth a lot of money.'

'What do we do then?' said Susan. 'Do we wait? Do we hang back, then go in and search this place after they've gone?'

'I say we get close now. I say we at least try to clock what it is they're hiding or meeting here for. There's only the four of them. So either somebody else is in there and we need to find out who that person is, or they've found the girl and they're keeping her hidden away here. Or it's a stash of something. Either way, we need to see if they're talking to someone.'

'Maybe we should phone Hope. Just clear it.'

'This is your call. You're the one who's got on to these people. Trust yourself,' said Perry.

'Let's go look then,' said Susan. 'Are you good at this?'

'They don't call me twinkle toes for nothing.'

'They don't call you twinkle toes at all.'

'No, but I know my limits,' said Perry. 'I can get close. If I'm going to get to a point where I can't get myself out of the way quick enough, I'll not do it. But you're smaller. You've got the physique. I reckon you'll have no problems.'

Susan gave Perry a smile and together the two crept forward towards the chapel. There was a set of large wooden doors at the front but they were fairly pointless as the windows in the old chapel had no wooden shutters in them. It was an old building, not without its pleasing aesthetic, but here in the night's cold, the stonework seemed barren. A strange place for people to be. Susan crept down low, Perry following.

'You stay here,' she said to Perry. 'I'll get up close. If there's any trouble, call for backup.'

Perry nodded, and Susan crept forward, hunkered down below the line of open windows. As she got closer, she stood up slowly, peering in through the gap.

Susan fought to stop herself from letting out a gasp. The

71

four men were standing almost in a circle. Straight up in the middle of them was a naked woman. She was shaking her head as they pointed at her, asking her questions in a language Susan didn't understand. There were slaps. She was hit across the face and on other parts of her body. There was nothing sexual about it. It was more of an angry group. Susan feared for the woman's safety. She hunkered back down and quickly made her way back to Perry.

'She's in there, surrounded by the four of them. Also naked. She's obviously struggled since she left the house.'

'We'll call for backup,' said Perry.

'But couldn't they go any time? They're also hitting her. We need to stop it. Who knows how far they'll go? Maybe she's at risk, then. Maybe.'

Perry nodded while he was working his phone and then said quietly, 'Backup has been called for. Let's go.' He stood up along with Susan, showing he would stand by the front doors. Susan walked around the side before sticking her head in through one of the open windows.

The men turned to bolt. Susan noticed that the front door had one half of it open, and as the first man arrived, the door shut quickly, catching him in the face. The door then opened, and she saw Perry step in with a nightstick.

He told the men to halt, to go down on their knees, but the first one stepped forward. Perry bent to one side and caught him with his nightstick on the side of the legs. Susan, meanwhile, hauled herself up to the open window, let herself drop, and ran over to the woman. She indicated the woman should go to the far wall and Susan walked quickly towards Perry.

He was now engaged by the three men and Susan took the

first of them from behind, kicking him in hard behind the knees and dropping him to the ground. She slapped some cuffs on him and quickly assessed the first one who'd hit the door. He was out cold. Perry had now taken a punch to the face and was reeling backwards somewhat and, Susan saw him take his jacket off. The man in front of him now pulled a knife.

Susan called for Perry to watch out and then ducked as a punch was swung towards her by the other, still-standing attacker. She stepped inside of him and pulled him down to the ground quickly. Perry had wrapped his coat around the hand of the man with the knife, covering the knife up. Susan jumped back up from her attacker, grabbing the other man's spare arm, driving it up towards his back and putting him down on his knees. Perry cuffed him, removing his coat and letting the knife drop to the ground. Perry stood over the men with a nightstick.

'Go to her,' he said. 'Give her your jacket. We're about to have many people come in here. She shouldn't be seen like that.'

'You sure you don't need me to cover here with you? There's four of them, Perry.'

'They move, and I'll batter them,' he said. 'Look after the woman.'

Susan strode quickly over to the woman, who was shaking in the corner. She whipped her jacket off, put it around the woman, closing it up from the front. A couple of minutes later, sirens could be heard, and a couple of constables rushed in.

'How many more have we got coming?' asked Perry.

'Three more cars on their way.'

'Good. Have them taken to the nearest station and down to the cells. Lock them up tight. Put some people on the cell door too, out in front of them.'

Susan threw him a look. He walked over to her. 'We got a hit. But who knows how deep these people are involved, or what they know?'

'Good idea. Let's get her in the car. I think we'll take her to Hope.'

'Good,' said Perry. 'We could be in for a long night.'

The woman looked up at Perry, almost afraid, but he smiled at her. 'Good now,' he said. 'You're good now. Safe. No bad men.'

Susan wasn't sure if she understood exactly what he said, at least not the words, but he said it in such a comforting tone. As she led the woman away to her car, she saw Perry hauling one man to the police car. He handled him roughly. But Susan noticed that he was out of sight of the rest.

Perry obviously had a lot of experience, but he also clearly had a lot of anger towards these men. It made her think about when he first joined the group. There's a lot more to think of about Perry, a lot more. He handled himself in the way Clarissa did, bravely. Fighting dirty, almost.

She came over to the car once the men were being transported away in police cars. 'Are we ready to go?' she asked, glancing at the woman in the rear.

'She thinks I might need a quick cigarette,' laughed Perry.

'She might want one herself,' said Susan. 'Quick one. You did good, Perry. Thanks for your help.'

'All your work,' he said. 'Don't worry, I'll make sure the boss knows.'

Chapter 10

Perry and Susan took the woman to the same accommodation the other women were being kept in. It was, however, five in the morning and the other women were sleeping. Perry thought it was a good idea to keep this woman separate, and he took her through to the kitchen. Susan went rummaging through the clothes that had been donated to the other women to find something suitable. Bringing them back to the kitchen, she let Perry depart for a moment. When he came back in, the woman had changed and the three of them sat down. Perry made the coffee for them all.

'Do you understand what I am saying?' asked Perry.

'A little,' said the woman.

'You didn't speak to us before. Why?'

'Afraid,' the woman said.

'We are police,' said Perry. He pulled out his warrant card and laid it down in front of the woman. 'Detective Constable Perry. This is Detective Constable Susan Cunningham. Me, Perry. This, Susan. What is your name?'

The woman looked at him for a moment, then picked up his badge, looking at it in detail. She placed it back down. 'Laura,' she said.

'Good,' said Perry. 'Coffee, Laura? You like the coffee?'

The woman nodded again.

'Can you say why you are here?'

Laura shook her head.

'Probably best if we get the translators,' said Susan. 'She's likely to speak one of the languages the other women speak.'

'I'm going to take a photo and get the other women up and talk to them,' announced Perry.

'Why?'

'Just a hunch. This woman ran off for a reason. I want to know why.'

'By the way, Perry,' asked Susan. 'What's your take on her age?'

Perry blew his cheeks out. 'I don't know. I mean, I doubt she's twenty. But if you told me she was fifteen, I wouldn't be surprised. That being said, she could be eighteen, nineteen. She looks young to me.'

'I think so. We might need to get an advocate.'

'Might need to get an advocate for all of them. We'll see.'

After taking a quick photograph of Laura, Perry stepped aside in the room and placed a call through to the translators. It was clear from the conversation that they'd been woken up, but Perry wanted them in now. He was polite about it, but he was firm, too.

It took about forty minutes for them to get in. Perry then woke the other women up, gathering them all together in their rooms. Susan called for a female police constable to come and sit with Laura while she joined Perry. He was sitting in one of the rooms with a translator speaking to one woman. The photograph of Laura was up on his phone.

'What are you doing?' asked Susan.

'They're all confirming that Laura was there. She's one of them, which we kind of guessed. She was the one a lot of them said was missing. This woman here, though, she's not so sure.'

'What do you mean she's not so sure? What did she say?'

'She said nothing,' said Perry. 'I was sitting here and the question was asked. She answered with her eyes. She looked away, and didn't answer properly.'

'And?' said Susan.

'We're just about to question her one to one.'

Perry held the phone up in front of the woman opposite. She was possibly Vietnamese, Susan thought. Certainly Asian, and very unlike some of the other women. Laura was white European. This woman stood out somewhat.

'Is this the woman you were talking about who disappeared?' Perry asked. The translator repeated the question. The woman looked away again.

'Ask her who she was thinking of. She wasn't thinking of this woman.' The female translator nodded. The translator's eyes were bleary, clearly being awoken from a decent slumber. And in fairness, the translators had worked hard the previous day. But Perry was on to something. Susan was sure of it.

'Get her to answer the question. She clearly has somebody else in mind.'

The woman spoke suddenly.

'She says that she knows nothing. She says Laura's the woman she was talking about.'

'Utter crap,' said Perry. He turned and looked at Susan, who could see the cogs ticking in his mind. Then he turned back to the woman.

'Tell her I have the four men who were looking after them.

The four men who have been pimping them. The men who have been making them commit sex acts with people. Tell them we have them. We have them locked up. And then tell her, if she doesn't start cooperating, she's going to be part of that. I need her to talk to me, to tell me everything she knows, so that I can get her out of this mess and off somewhere sensible. Somewhere where she can have a decent life. At the moment, she's cutting her own throat.'

The translator looked at him.

'Put that in a better way,' he said. He looked at Susan, who was doing her best not to laugh.

'It's English. That's what we say.'

'They might take it a bit different though,' said Susan. The translator nodded.

The woman spoke back after a moment and then she kept talking. Susan went to interrupt but Perry put his hand up, indicating Susan should let the woman finish. She spoke for almost a minute.

'She says that's not the woman she was thinking of. The hair colour's wrong. The woman also wasn't Asian. She says she didn't really know Laura at all.'

'Who was the other woman then?'

'She says she didn't know her. They don't always stay together in the same groups, although there's a big number of them; they've been brought separately. This woman wasn't from her group, but she saw her at the house.'

'Okay,' said Perry. 'I'm going to wake up more people and get a sketch artist in. We're going to get a picture of this other woman.'

'Good idea,' said Susan. 'And then we can show it to Laura.'

'Absolutely,' said Perry. 'And between that, I'm going to do something else.'

'What?' asked Susan.

'I'm going to smoke a couple of fags. I'm going to get some breakfast. You got some sleep, remember? I was the one watching the guys.'

'You get your fags after your phone call. I'll make the breakfast,' said Susan.

It took the sketch artist about an hour to arrive. During that time, Susan had cooked some sausages, bacon, and some eggs from the accommodation the women were staying in. Perry sat down and tucked into them. The bitter smell of smoke from his copious cigarettes outside was evident on his clothing.

'Do you ever think about giving them up?' asked Susan.

'What do you mean?' asked Perry.

'The cigs. Do you ever think about giving them up?'

'Why?'

'You realise you're actually quite—well, there's something about you, Perry, but the cigs are very off-putting.'

'Are you flirting with me?' he asked.

'No, no,' said Susan. 'We're not going there. What I'm saying is that you turn up and people smell the cigarettes and they get this complete image of Perry as the old dinosaur. But you're a clever sausage, aren't you? You're actually cultured in your own way. Got a hell of a brain on you.'

'Has Hope been asking you to build me up? Has she been saying she's been treating me rough or something?'

Susan laughed. 'Seriously. I think you should give up the cigarettes. I think you would—well, I think you'd do all right.'

Perry threw her a smile. 'Okay,' he said. 'I'll have a think about that. In the context of this conversation, I'll not tell you that you cook a mean breakfast, one I'd love to sample a lot more.'

Susan punched him on the arm. 'That's outrageous,' she said.

He laughed. 'It's just a joke.'

'I know,' she said. 'I know.'

When the sketch artist arrived, Perry took him through and got the translator to help with getting a description of the woman Laura had seen. When the picture was finished, Laura waved at Perry, clearly wanting to say more.

'Let her speak,' said Perry. 'Tell her to talk away.'

The translator took down notes of what was being said. After a couple of minutes, Laura stopped and looked over at Perry. The translator turned to him and Susan.

'Blimey. Okay, she said that the woman was with Laura that night. Donal took a fancy to both of them and took them both into his bedroom. She then gave some detail about various sexual acts, which I've noted, but you can run through them later if you want. But the guts of it is, she was there with Laura. She went to sleep after doing a lot of this stuff. When Laura woke up, she saw Donal missing. The woman was missing, too. She went out and found Donal in the recording studio. She said somebody was there. There was a person there, but she didn't see who. She looked at him and thought he was dead.'

'Ask her if there was a fire.'

'She says she didn't notice one. But she ran. That's when she disappeared off.'

'And she went because—'

The translator asked, and the woman replied.

'She says would you believe her if he was found dead? She said she's like a prostitute. Would you believe a prostitute? So, she ran and hid. She said people came looking for her, but she hid from them. Despite being cold in the night, she had to keep out of sight because she had no clothing. And then she got spotted by those men again. The keepers, she's calling them. I think that's the best description.'

'Keepers?'

'As in like zookeeper,' said the translator. 'Yeah. It's not good.'

'I want you to go through everything with her. Everything. And write it down in a statement. Put it in her language, so she can sign it, to show what happened. And do out the translation as well,' said Perry. 'I'll leave you to that for a couple of hours. Tell her to tell you as much as she can.'

Perry left the room with Susan and then picked up the phone. He called Hope.

'Perry,' she said, 'what's been going on?'

'Cunningham found her woman. We've got her in with the translators. She was legging it because she woke up and found Donal was dead. Basically she'd gone to have sex with him the previous night along with another woman. This other woman was missing. I think we could have a hit on our hands and that woman may be the person who did it. I'm getting a description. A sketch artist can then draw it up and we'll try to find out who did this.'

'Do you think our hitwoman is on the loose? Do you think she knows?'

'She's got to know that she was seen with the group. Now if she's gone in with Laura, our new-found girl, to Donal, well, then I'm surprised she didn't finish her. Although—'

'What?'

'Maybe it didn't go to plan. Maybe she got disturbed. Did Fags interrupt her? There's a story here we're not seeing.'

'Okay, Perry,' said Hope. 'I'll call Macleod. This is taking on arms and legs, I think. In fact, Perry, remain on the line. I'm going to patch him in.'

'You going to do a three-way call with him?'

'You sound sceptical,' said Hope.

'I do. Ross is here. I've heard about the boss's lack of technological know-how.'

It took ten minutes before Macleod entered the three-way call. He gave a bit of a cough.

'You all sorted, Seoras?' asked Hope.

'Sorry, yes. Just a bit of an issue. I think the phone's playing up. Jane sorted it.'

'Of course,' said Hope. She brought Macleod up to speed on what Perry was saying,

'So you think definitely a hit, Perry?'

'I do,' he said. 'I think Hope concurs.'

'Definitely,' said Hope, 'this is a hit; this is a targeted killing.'

'Well, you've got your work cut out,' said Macleod. 'I'm coming down.'

'To take over?' said Hope. 'That's not—'

'No,' said Macleod, 'I'm coming down because you need some cover. You've got the four of you, you've got a mass of people to coordinate with, and you're going to have the press jumping all over it. I noticed Ross was doing the last lot of press coverage. We're going to have to be very careful with what we put out and how we do it. They will not take it coming from a detective sergeant. They're going to want to have a name up there. Well, they're not having the glamour girl, they're going to get the grumpy git instead. I'm coming down to give you a hand,' said Macleod.

'Still your investigation, Hope, and you're still going to get to the bottom of it. But I'll run cover for you; keep these press dogs off your back. I'll be down by lunchtime.'

'Very good, sir,' said Hope. She realised he'd left the call, and Perry was still there.

'That's a vote of confidence if ever I heard one,' said Perry. Hope stopped herself for a minute. What did he mean by that? She realised Perry was being quite genuine.

'It is,' said Hope. 'So we need to sort this out. We need to find that contracted killer. Back to it, Perry. You and Susan go find her for me.'

Perry came off the phone call and looked across at Susan. 'The big boss is coming down to run cover. I think Hope's just have been told to get to the bottom of it. You and me too. So let's get on with it.'

Susan smiled, then left the room leaving Perry alone with his phone. *Well, well,* he thought. *Things are looking up for this team. Maybe I can get off the fags. Maybe.*

Chapter 11

Hope wanted to stand outside, finding the interior of the appropriated rooms for the investigation a little stuffy. However, the press were out there and they'd take photographs of her—the forlorn inspector as they would describe it. She also didn't want Macleod arriving and her being seen to greet him outside. She could see the headlines now—'battered inspector welcomes old genius.'

Of course, that's not what Macleod was doing, but it never stopped the papers or the media from reporting it for the way they liked. She tried to stay off the media, tried not to look at it when a case was on. After all, especially one like this, in which the victim was a media junkie. He was a rock star. And he was the sort of star people loved to hate or love with no middle ground. A divisive man, indulging his very dubious preferences.

Macleod's car turned into the car park where it parked up amid a flash of photography. He stepped out in a long coat, dressed as usual in a suit and tie, and walked towards completely the wrong building. Hope thought she was going to have to step out, but fortunately a constable put his hand up, showing that the DCI should move a different direction.

Macleod smiled at the man, before arriving at the door behind which stood Hope. He opened it, stepped through, and give her a broad smile.

'Sorry, I didn't want to meet you out there. Too many—'

'Yes, yes, yes,' said Macleod, 'too many photographers. I hope you're appreciating this. I'm here to deal with them.'

'I hope you're in a good mood. You're not going to—'

'Excuse me; I said I'm coming to help.'

'Yes, but you never liked them,' said Hope. 'You always sent me out to them.'

'That's because I was thinking. That's because my mind needed space. This is your investigation, and you need space. So, space is what I'm providing.'

'I'm doing an update meeting. I hung on until you arrived, thought it best for you to be in with the team.'

'Grand,' he said. 'I take it there's a cup of coffee waiting.'

Hope didn't actually know if there was a cup of coffee waiting. She didn't answer, but guided Macleod to the meeting room. On opening the door, she saw a cup of coffee sitting, steaming, on the table. Everyone else's was half drunk.

'Excellent,' said Macleod. He took off his coat, hung it up, and walked across to sit down. He noted his seat was at the head of the table. Macleod moved the coffee round and then swapped seats before sitting down.

'Head of the table's yours,' he said to Hope. 'I'm the DCI. I'm not the senior investigating officer. You're running the investigation. That's your place.'

Hope gave him a nod and then turned to the rest of the team. 'Right. Let's get on then. Seems to me that there's a contract killer involved here. And we think it may be this woman.' Hope pointed to a picture stuck up on the whiteboard. It had been sketched earlier on in the day from the description given by Laura.

'Laura was part of the group of women brought in to entertain Donal Diamond and Larry Goodlad. Allegedly, Donal Diamond organised this. We've currently got four men who provided the women, locked up in cells here but refusing to speak. We'll have to get into that. However, the contracted killer wasn't with the ladies. Is that right, Perry?'

'Yes,' said Perry. 'I've used the translators, talking to all the women. They were divided off into two groups before they arrived here, and neither group had seen this woman.'

'So how does that work?' asked Cunningham. 'She what, just pitches up?'

'Just slips in. She must have known,' said Hope. 'She must have known that the women wouldn't know each other.'

'But what's the plan?' asked Perry.

'Hold that for a moment,' said Hope. 'Jona, confirm what you know.'

'Donal Diamond was poisoned with cyanide. It was delivered professionally, simply. No mess, no fuss into his system. He probably didn't even know it was being administered. By the sounds of it, he was paralytic. He's got enough booze and drugs in his system to have floored him. And he'd also had a lot of sexual activity that day.'

'Really not the most pleasant of people, is he?' said Macleod.

'Outside of that, the fire was set deliberately. The ignition source was a flame brought in from external efforts. We're not sure if it could have been some sort of blowtorch or could indeed have been a basic light. The fire spread reasonably quickly. What I do know is that Donal Diamond was placed on a chair after he'd been poisoned. His guitar positioned in front of him and he was dead while the fire burned.'

Hope nodded. 'We don't have a positive ID but I'm suspecting our contract killer was the one that placed him there. Laura, our runaway woman, says that she was taken into a bedroom along with this contracted killer for sex with Donal Diamond. Everyone passed out as far as Laura knew. She awoke, and he wasn't there. Laura padded her way over towards the recording studio and found him sitting upright. She thought there was someone else in there, but she legged it as fast as she could.'

'Smart girl,' said Macleod. 'Otherwise, she'd be dead.'

'Exactly,' said Perry. 'And she was smart enough to stay hidden. She didn't know who her enemy was. But she was then picked up by our four cohorts that brought the women here. And Susan rescued her from them.'

'That's a bit of overkill, Perry. You did have your hand in it. A large hand,' said Susan.

'It's not important,' said Perry. 'Point is, Susan's search worked. And she also had us keeping tabs on these four guys. That's how we got Laura back. I think Laura needs to be under good protection.'

'I agree with that,' said Susan. 'We've got guards on the women, but we are talking a contract killer.'

'I'd double it up,' said Macleod. 'Make sure they are teams of people who know each other. What's the reason for putting a contract killer on him?'

'Could be the inheritance,' said Hope. 'He's worth an absolute packet.'

'What about the family, then? We looked into them?'

'Evangeline and Tee-Tee. Evangeline's his estranged wife and left him when she was a couple of years with Tee-Tee. Prior to that she said she was good with his copious sex and having groupies around all the time. She was spending as much time as she could with Tee-Tee and his money. He was doing what he did. She didn't care. When she had Tee-Tee, she wanted Tee-Tee to have a better life, not have a dad who she walked in on having sex with the groupies.'

'Fine bred woman then,' said Macleod.

'I wouldn't go that far. Tee-Tee's now a teenager, just turned eighteen, I think. In therapy every week. And she saw her father not long before the murder, so she's well aware of what he does. She said the women were there already, apparently walking around the place in the scunner.'

'In the nude,' said Macleod, 'for those who don't come from Glasgow.'

'There is another side to it,' said Hope. 'Ross has been looking into people who have claimed that Donal Diamond was their father. They would have a claim on inheritance.'

'Do we actually have a will?' asked Macleod

'No, It's quite shocking isn't it' said Hope. 'It would make things a lot clearer but at the moment everything would go to Tee-Tee. Possibly also to any of these other claims. There are, however, sixty individuals, according to the papers and other malarkey who could be siblings of Tee-Tee, albeit half siblings.'

'What about his wife? Is she divorced?'

'No, Seoras' said Hope. 'She is, however, estranged. She has a typewritten contract that gave her money and she's not in the inheritance and will not look for it.'

'That's all signed and sealed?'

'Check that,' said Ross. 'Button tight. Don't believe she's involved in it.'

'How's she live?' asked Macleod.

'Well,' said Hope. 'Very well. She doesn't really want for anything. It's the old question, though. How much money is enough? For some people, having a bit to do a bit is enough.'

'Did she look like that person?'

'Hard to say,' said Hope. 'She looked comfortable where she was. She seemed to have genuine concern for Tee-Tee but would she want more?'

'You'd have to have money to make a contract killing though, wouldn't you?' said Perry. 'I'm not that au fait with them, but you'd have to have a bit of cash.'

'Who's got cash then? Who's got enough money to do it? Music bigwigs?' asked Macleod.

'Well, I don't know,' said Hope. 'Would the record companies really be involved? Would it really affect them? I mean, the money, the estate going to someone doesn't affect them, does it? They're still making the money.'

'If I can just interject with something,' said Macleod. 'I had a look at how well his records are doing since he's been dead.'

'It's not really been that long, has it?' said Perry.

'No, but they're through the roof. You lot may have been deeply engaged down here but you're obviously not checking the charts as a man like me would do.'

'The charts? I think the charts went out a while ago.'

'Not the download ones, Ross,' said Macleod, 'I'm not that much of a dinosaur. He's making a lot of money, or sorry, his estate's making a lot of money, but also other record companies who he used to work for. This death is big business. Consider that angle too. I hear he was a lot of trouble.'

'Sex, booze, drugs, all the usual,' said Hope.

'Yes,' said Macleod, 'the usual is not the same anymore. Back in the 70s, 80s, these people had a persona that worked.

Nowadays, the images are a lot cleaner. Being dead, being something that's a tale from the past, may sell better records than being seen with a bunch of naked women in the present.'

'Okay,' said Hope. 'That's taken on board. We'll look into that.'

'Another thing,' said Ross. 'We know little about his early life, do we? He was in an orphanage.'

'That sounds like something up your street,' said Hope. 'Get into that. Find out where he came from. If we're looking at inheritance claims, we're going to have to look everywhere. Discover where he came from. If the daughter is the obvious one, and she is in the way of less obvious claimants, somebody has used a contract killer once, they may use them twice. We need to establish these ideas quickly.'

'Should we bring her under protection, then?' asked Perry. 'We need to find this mysterious killer, don't you think? Could put the daughter under protection, though.'

'Tee-Tee would have to agree to that, and she would also have to abide by our rules,' said Hope. 'We can do it. But one, it may let people know you're on to them. Two, she might not agree to it. And three, what are we going to do with her and for how long? Foremost, we need to find out who the contract killer is and get on top of them. You need to solve this by finding out who hired them.'

'To do that, we need all the connections,' said Susan.

'True,' said Hope. She walked over to the whiteboard and stood, looking at the image that had been drawn of the contract killer. She turned back to Susan. 'You were good with the guys. You were able to find our runaway,' said Hope. 'I think you need something else to get your teeth into.' Susan looked up a little questioningly.

'Susan, I want you to find this woman, this killer. I want you to find out who she is, how she operated, and where she is now. Okay?'

'Okay,' said Susan, 'I haven't had an awful lot of experience with—'

'No, you haven't. Perry, you're with her. You've got the experience, haven't you? You've seen some things like this before. I know you said you hadn't dealt with many contract killers but you've seen enough?'

'Perry's got the experience,' said Macleod. 'It's a good call.' At that point, he went silent, leaving Hope waiting for something else to be said. But he was offering nothing. She took up her rallying call again.

'Perry will have ideas of where, how, what. You've got the ingenuity to keep going at it. You also can go at things much more than I can. I'm tied to here. It's not Ross's strength. He'll get into the computers. Dig out who these people are, Susan.

'I'll stay based around here. Unless I am needed anywhere. Seoras is going to cover off the media. If you get any issues from the media, you fire it at Seoras. If you get any trouble from the media, you fire it at Seoras. Seoras is going to make sure that the media behaves. He's going to feed them with the banal tat that we want them fed with.'

Macleod put up his hand. 'What is banal tat? I'm going to give them informative, useful statements which they can print in their paper. By the way, who does the coffee these days?'

Susan put her hand up.

'It's not a complaint, but if you check with Ross, just black. There's a wee drop of milk in there I didn't want.'

'Unless it's a proper one,' said Ross; 'then he wants a latte. And then—'

'I didn't ask for the explanation, Ross,' said Macleod. 'Your boss has given you something to do. Off you go.' The team stood up and as Susan walked past, Macleod gave her a nod, 'but thank you for the thought. It's appreciated.' They disappeared out of the room and Macleod saw Hope staring after them.

'What's up?' he asked.

'Have I done the right thing with Susan? She's still quite young, still quite—'

'Susan's a trooper, and she's got Perry with her. How did they apprehend the men, anyway? Perry said Susan did it.'

'Susan said that Perry had his nightstick. Had two of them taken down before she could help him.'

'And he went against four? With a nightstick?'

'Hit the first with the door.'

Macleod laughed. 'That sounds about right. Good job she helped him, though. He wouldn't have lasted against four. He's not a proper fighter, not like you and Susan.'

'She seems quite taken with him,' said Hope.

'Good. At least somebody's on his side.'

'I have been better with him. I've brought him in. He's doing good. He looked after the women well with not one saucy comment.'

'Told you he's a good one. Keep listening to that brain of his. It's good, it's very good. He'll see stuff you don't.'

'Thank you, but I've got work to do,' said Hope. She gave Macleod a smile. 'And so have you. Get at them press boys for me.'

'I meant to ask you,' said Macleod. 'Obviously, this shirt-tie combo of mine doesn't cut the mustard. Jeans and T-shirt? How do you work a figure in front of the media?'

Hope threw him a punch on the arm. 'Get out,' she said.

As he walked to the door, he turned back. 'Doing okay,' Macleod said. 'Still early days, but get after that killer. She could be very dangerous.'

Chapter 12

I t didn't take Ross long to locate the orphanage, and he jumped into the car, making a beeline for Edinburgh. His note said that Donal had been brought up there, a Catholic charity back in the day, and Ross wondered exactly what he would meet. The orphanage was located close to the town centre. As Ross parked up and walked around the Edinburgh streets looking at some of the great sandstone buildings, he used his mapping feature to arrive at a small placard on the sandstone wall.

St Bernard's was looking a little worse for wear. The windows had a long time since been replaced. But now they had plastic on the outside and the plastic had taken on that worn look. Dark smudges running through the white. The windows looked like they hadn't been cleaned in a long while.

He climbed the steps, noticing that several of them were chipped, and reached a large, wooden door with some glass panels in it. He looked through to see a rather dark hallway beneath. Ross looked around for a doorbell. Finding none, he tried the handle, and the door opened, letting him through to the vestibule inside.

Once there, he stood looking around and realised there was

a small bell sitting on a table. He descended upon it with his hand and the ring echoed along the tall stairs in front of him and into the rooms on either side. A woman almost shuffled out, wearing a nun's habit.

'Hello?' she said.

'Hi, my name's Detective Sergeant Ross. I'm with Police Scotland, Inverness. I'm on the investigation into the death of Donal Diamond.'

'Right,' said the woman.

'Do you know who he is?' asked Ross.

'Yes,' said the woman, almost annoyed at the insinuation she wouldn't.

'Well, I'd like to know some details about him.'

'He's a rock star, as far as I know,' said the woman. 'I don't know where he lives. He had several records, well, quite a few. His last, though, was a few years ago. He's had several singles.'

'No, no, no, no. I mean, about his early life.'

The nun looked at him, bemused. 'Why would you ask me about that? I never knew the man. My brother was into that sort of music a long time ago. That's how I know what I do. That and we occasionally have to read the papers.'

'This is an orphanage, isn't it?'

'No longer,' said the sister. 'We stopped being an orphanage ten years ago.'

'What is it then?' asked Ross. 'Sign still says Bernard's orphanage outside.'

'It's an old placard. Never really had the money or the funds to replace it with something else.'

'So what is it?'

'Well, some of us nuns occupy it now. We work with the city mission here in Edinburgh. This is our accommodation.'

'You left the front door open. You've got a bell here.'

'Yes,' said the sister. 'There's no other way of communicating around. One of us usually is in prayer, or doing some works around here, so if anyone comes to call we sort them out.'

'Would there be any records from the orphanage?'

'I think there would be, yes. Let me think.'

'What's your name, by the way?' asked Ross.

'Sister Mary.'

Of course, Sister Mary. Narrowing her down to one of only several billion nuns around the world with that name.

Ross was fidgety. He'd called his son the previous night, and he wasn't happy that dad was still staying away. Angus had tried to put a bright spin on it, telling him what his son had done that day. All the minor triumphs, but Ross was missing it. Ross was not being allowed to see it. All because of some guy who got smacked up on drugs, had sex with copious women, and then got himself killed over money. Ross couldn't help but feel that he was losing his drive for the job these days. He wanted to do something else, didn't he?

'You there? Sorry, was it Inspector?'

'No, Detective Sergeant. Detective Sergeant Ross, Sister.'

'Yes, I was just saying, Sister Bernadette would be the one to talk to. Rather old. Can I fetch her?'

'Of course,' said Ross. He stood there waiting while Sister Mary disappeared up the stairs. Five minutes later, she came down.

'I'm afraid Sister Bernadette's not in a great way today. She's quite old, so some days she's better than others, but she's not managed the stairs today. Can I ask, would you come up to see her?'

'Of course,' said Ross, and followed Sister Mary up a spiralling staircase. It was grandiose, old style, and went up four floors.

'Are all these floors used for rooms for yourself and the sisters?'

'Yes. Yes.'

'May I venture why Sister Bernadette is at the top if she's struggling with the stairs?'

'Because that's where she wants to be. I'm afraid you shouldn't try to work out nuns. We're different. Sister Bernadette's been up there for, oh, years. It used to be when it was an orphanage that all the sisters were up the top, except for whoever was doing the night duty downstairs on the door. She's never given her room up.'

'She's been here the whole time.'

'Been here for fifty years,' said Sister Mary, 'at least, as far as I can work out. She is in her nineties.'

Ross continued to traipse up the stairs, eventually coming to a room at the top. A simple door opened, and he saw an elderly woman sitting in a chair. There was a bed beside her, a small writing desk, but little else.

'This is Sister Bernadette. Sister Bernadette,' said Sister Mary. Her voice was raised suddenly, and Sister Bernadette put up a hand, Ross wondering how long she could keep it there for. The woman was dressed in the usual nun's habit, her hair covered, but the face said her life had been a hard one. However, she gave a smile, in as much as she could, her gums showing because the teeth weren't there.

'The sister's hard of hearing,' said Sister Mary. 'You might have to talk loudly to her.'

'Hello,' said Ross. 'I'm Detective, Detective Sergeant Ross.'

'Ross? Sergeant,' said Sister Bernadette. 'Inspector.' Sister

Bernadette pointed to Sister Mary.

'I got that wrong,' laughed Sister Mary. 'It's Detective Sergeant Ross. He wants to ask you some questions.'

'Not good enough for an inspector.' The old woman spat.

Just answer the questions, thought Ross. *I don't need this.*

'I want to talk about a Donal Diamond. Do you know Donal Diamond?'

The woman turned and almost spat again towards the floor.

Ross looked over at Sister Mary. 'We don't always behave as we should when we get older,' said Sister Mary quietly. 'But she'll answer your questions.'

'I need to know about Donal Diamond when he came here.'

'Donal Diamond? The sister shook her head.

'Are you able to answer questions like that?' said Ross.

'I'm a little old,' said the nun suddenly. 'But I'm not insane, and I'm not senile. I might be a touch bitter; God forgive me. Donal Diamond used to be Donal Finnegan.'

'And he lived here?' asked Ross.

'Hold your horses, I'm getting to that. Donal Finnegan was a decent lad. Donal Diamond is the incarnation of the devil. Sex, sex, sex,' said the old woman. It was rather disturbing to Ross the way she spoke about it. 'That sort of thing. We all dream, we all get carried away. I've had my moments.' Ross tried not to think about that. 'But, his behaviour—he'll meet his God. Because he was one of us. He was warned. He was told.'

'I appreciate that,' said Ross, 'but—'

'Are you okay?' the nun asked. 'We're never ready to meet him. We're never ready. And today has gone so wrong. Everybody with their lifestyles. I hope you're not promiscuous.'

'No,' answered Ross truthfully.

'Got a pleasant woman at home? Got a son?'

It isn't wasn't worth the effort, Ross thought. There was a time when he would have proudly told her that Angus was his husband. But there was no point now. He needed information from this woman about Donal Diamond. Not to have her start accusing him of being the devil or something worse.

'I have a son.'

'Good. Donal Finnegan came here when his mother was taken away. Three of them. Three kids left behind. Father died, and the mother was taken to a mental institute, but she died six months later. The three of them were Donal, Rosheen and Fergus. Good Irish Christian names. Rosheen and Fergus, however, were twins, two years older. They were here for all their child life. Started off out into Edinburgh. Once they left, we kept tabs with Rosheen and Fergus. Rosheen died.'

'How?' asked Ross.

'Hit and run. Car hit her somewhere in Edinburgh. Didn't stop. Waste. Good girl. Fergus was cut up but he never stayed after that. Never kept in touch. He was gone. Donal found fame and wrote to us. We warned him about what he was doing but he found fame so quickly. He came back here once, but you couldn't have him around the kids here and around the sisters. Some of the younger sisters they get—well, it's difficult to choose this life. They want someone, and sometimes you don't know if you want someone, or not. Best at that time not to have the temptation. Best to work it out.'

'And then Donal found his fame.'

'It was in the paper. Pictures of him. Back in the days when papers could do that, you know. They had photos of, well, nudity. Nowadays, they all have to cover up, don't they? They can't show it. They showed some back then, because, of course, they had people posing back then, didn't they? Some say the world's got worse, but maybe the papers have got better. But Donal Diamond, he's the devil.'

'Any idea where Fergus went?'

'Fergus Finnegan was the quiet one. Rosheen was the nice one,' said the nun. 'But Fergus vanished.'

'Well, thank you,' said Ross. He'd have to find Fergus. Fergus Finnegan; he might be hard enough to find if he was even still alive. Donal might have known, or maybe he hadn't.

Sister Mary escorted Ross back down the steps of the building into the vestibule where she stood for a moment expectantly.

'Is there anything else you can add . . . or any records?'

'You can check the records online,' said the sister. She disappeared and brought back a card.

'Number on here will give you the people who deal with our records. I hope she's been of help to you, Sister Bernadette, and I hope she didn't offend you.'

'Offend me?' said Ross.

'Yes. Offend you. Talk of children and things. And about people and lifestyles.'

'Why would it offend me?' asked Ross.

'You have a husband. You talked about the child, but you never mentioned your wife. I've found talking to men of your persuasion that when they're under pressure, they do either one of two things. They either announce it proudly or they try to just keep it out of the conversation. I appreciate you're doing a job at the moment, so I'm sorry if she made you feel uncomfortable.'

'Are you going to tell me that the church—'

'We are a varied bunch these days. We must deal with a lot of changes. Some of us are changing with it. Some of us have determined that the old things should stay. I won't pretend I know who's right.'

Ross put his hand over and shook the nun's hand. 'Well, thank you,' he said. 'Thank you for at least saying sorry.'

'If you need anything else beyond that number, feel free to come and call on me.'

Ross turned, left the building, still shaking his head about the nun he had met up the stairs.

Chapter 13

S usan decided to visit Laura again to see if she could find any more information about the contract killer. As they drove along in the car, Susan heard Perry whistling.

'What are you whistling for?'

'I don't know,' he said. 'Just feeling good. I was apprehensive about coming into this team. I'd worked with Macleod before and he's, well, you know what he's like. He can be quite officious, but he seems to take an offhand approach to the killer at the moment. Very much Hope's boat, isn't it?'

'Absolutely. I mean, they've put you and me onto the contract killer.'

'Yes. Hope obviously has a lot of faith in you.'

'Well, I got the feeling I would not get to do it except you were here.'

'Don't put yourself down,' said Perry.

'What is it you've done?'

'I've done quite a few things. Macleod knows. I just never went up the ranks. Never really got myself into gear. Macleod said I ruined myself.'

'Macleod said that to you?'

'Yeah, it was a few years ago now, but he was a little different then. When I knew him, he was very, very strait-laced. Very serious. But he had his own issues. He seems happier now. He didn't have that new woman he's got, though, either. What's she called?'

'Jane?'

'Yes. She wasn't around. In fact, he didn't have a woman.'

'Well, it's amazing what they can do for you.'

'What are you like?' said Perry. Susan smiled.

They approached the accommodation where the women were staying, and Susan noted that there were many police officers peering out from inside. She wasn't sure if it was good thing or not. Maybe they should have been in plain clothes. But then again, it would have been difficult to have kept this all a secret.

The women worked together, and this was keeping them away from the men who had used them. But did the idea of a contract killer mean that were more at risk? If they'd all seen this woman, then maybe they would be. But Laura was the one with the description. Laura was the one who had been in the room with Donal and had sex with him. And engaged in other actions with this female killer.

Susan pulled up in the car, stepped out, and walked over towards the door. Once she'd reached the door, two police officers came out and told her to keep her hands on show. They knew who she was, but they let her present her credentials anyway, maybe just in case they thought they were being tested. After Perry presented his warrant card, the pair were let inside. They made their way into the main living room of the accommodation block where a number of the women were sitting together. Perry saw some of the translators who were still working with them, taking down statements. He asked one of them if they'd seen Laura.

'I think she's upstairs asleep.'

'That makes sense. It's all been a bit of a toll on her.'

Perry advised Susan, and the two of them went upstairs. They opened the door of the woman's room gently, going past the officer who was standing outside. She was indeed completely asleep.

'Maybe we should let her stay for an hour,' said Perry. 'Why don't you keep an eye?'

'I know what you're up to,' said Susan. 'You're off for a fag. I've told you, give them up.'

'And I want you to know,' said Perry, 'that I've actually considered it, and I'm still considering it. That's how much you mean to me.'

Susan tried not to let out a laugh, in case she'd wake Laura.

'I'll stay in here then. Have your ciggy.'

Perry walked down the stairs and outside of the accommodation block. He took out a cigarette, lit up, and breathed in deeply. Giving them up would be tough. He'd had them for so long they were almost a part of him. The action of going to find a packet, of buying it, of making sure there was always one about was strangely therapeutic. He needed to give them up though—they would kill him eventually.

That was the bit he didn't understand about himself. He had this brain that some of them talked about. A man with an understanding, he could see things, but that the cigarettes would kill him in the future was an easy decision. Anybody could work that out, yet he still didn't give them up. Still, he thought, Susan really put a challenge to him, didn't she? Others had told him, but for some reason, coming from her seemed to carry more gravitas.

Perry turned and wandered round to the rear of the accommodation, puffing away, letting his mind wander. Sometimes he did his best thinking when that happened. And then he saw a woman walking around the back of the accommodation. There was a man emptying bins, and he walked over to him.

'Can I see your ID, sir?' he asked.

The man showed him. It was around his neck in a little plastic envelope.

'John,' said Perry, 'can you tell me who that is over there?'

'I don't know,' said John. 'I just do the bins and I don't do them that often. She might work here, she might not. I have no idea who she is.'

'Thank you, John.'

Perry watched the woman walking back and forth. He continued with his cigarette.

Susan Cunningham, he thought. *Why am I thinking about giving up cigarettes? Because Susan Cunningham said so. She's what, fifteen years my junior? Maybe more? She's attractive, but I'm not that shallow. I may blag in that way, a bit of banter, but deep down I'm never shallow. It's just a persona, a defence.*

Perry loved genuine conversation—deep, meaningful ideas being challenged. He didn't think that Susan was an airhead, but they hadn't been that deep in conversation yet. She had a way about her, though.

He grinned to himself as he drew in some more smoke. He looked round. The woman had gone. He took a couple of steps around the edge of the building and stepped back quickly. She was climbing up the rear fire escape. Perry turned the corner. He peered carefully and watched the woman.

She looked inside rooms as she made her way up. The woman seemed to count. That bothered Perry. She clearly

105

knew what she wanted to do. She didn't know the room, but she knew roughly where somebody was.

He picked up his phone and texted a message. The woman continued up the fire escape, eventually coming to the top floor. She was wrong there, then. If this was somebody after Laura, Laura was on the floor below. He almost texted again, to advise this, but instead, he let his original recommendation remain.

Carefully, Perry climbed the fire escape. He tried to be as gentle as possible, eventually getting up to the top floor. He edged his way along, feeling the sweat run down his face. As he peered round the corner of the window, looking into the room the woman had climbed into, he saw no one there. Thankfully, whoever's room it was must have been downstairs. The woman who had climbed up, however, was busy.

She was down on the floor. Perry saw her remove what looked like a compact drill, and she began to whir the smallest of holes into the floor. And then she took out a gun.

It had a long silencer on the front, and Perry's heart suddenly skipped a beat. He was up here, on the fire escape, while a woman he believed was the contract killer was in the room beside him, armed. There was nowhere to go if she came out of this window. By the time he got down from the fire escape, she'd have seen him, and no doubt she could shoot.

Perry edged his way back from the window and started checking the other windows. One was open slightly. He pushed it open fully. He was about to get inside when his curiosity got the better of him. Slowly, he edged back over to the original window the woman had gone through.

He peered around again and saw her with the gun pointing down through the floor. It was fired twice, with some barely audible puffs. As soon as she did that, Perry raced backwards. He climbed into the other room, closed the window behind him, and got down tight against the wall underneath the window. It would be hard to see him.

Carefully, he extracted a mirror on the end of an extendable pole, and moved it across to where it would be out of line of anyone looking in the window. But he could see at least a shadow falling from there, positioned by the window. It took another twenty seconds before he saw that shadow, someone looking in, above him. And then it was gone.

Perry counted to twenty before he lifted the window, sending the mirror up, checking no one was looking in. There wasn't. Quickly, Perry looked out of the window. The woman was on the ground floor of the fire escape.

She turned a corner, so he opened the window and climbed out. He tried to get down as quickly as he could, and as quietly as he could. He watched as the woman disappeared into a car and drove off.

Perry ran for the car. Starting it up, he drove with his phone out. He simply texted 'in pursuit' to Susan and kept driving.

The woman disappeared round country bends, but Perry kept up. Every time she disappeared from view, he increased the speed until he saw her, until at last she didn't reappear. He doubled back on himself because he had seen a country hotel. Parking his car somewhere down the driveway but not right into the car park beside the hotel's building, Perry walked up through some trees. He hunkered down and visually scanned the car park until he saw the car that the woman had used. He took out his phone and called Susan Cunningham.

'Susan,' he whispered. 'How is everything back there?'

'We're a bit shaken up,' said Susan. 'But we're okay. All alive.'

'Good. I've got her. Well, at least I know where she's staying.'

'Good,' said Susan, 'but we need to move Laura. She fired two shots into the pillow where Laura's head would have been. Fortunately enough, I had got her out and built up the duvet so it looked like a figure was there. The woman didn't wait to check the body.'

'Call Macleod and Hope. Ask them how they want to play this. Tell them I think we need to pretend she's dead. Have you shown her alive to anyone yet?'

'No,' said Susan. 'We hid in the wardrobe, and I brought her back out afterwards. We're still in the room.'

'Good,' said Perry. 'Stay there, don't come out, or rather, do go out; talk to the constable on duty. Get him to call Macleod and that inn, saying she's dead. Ask for Hope to come in to see you, organise it from there. You might need to put Jona in the loop as well.'

'Good idea. What are you going to do?'

'I'm going to sit here and make sure somebody doesn't leave.'

'Be careful. She's a contract killer. She'll know about people following her. Watch your back!'

'Then we better lift her from here before she gets out on the go again. Get moving, Susan. I don't enjoy sitting here like this. I'll be safer when backup arrives.'

'You sure you still want to give up smoking?' she said to Perry.

'I think you may have persuaded me.'

'Well, sitting here in this wardrobe and hearing those bullets hit the pillow, I felt like starting up!'

Chapter 14

Hope stood shaking her head in the accommodation the women were staying in. She had just broken the bad news to them all about the death of Laura. Preparations were being made by Jona's people to take the body away, for Jona had been in there for the last four or five hours. What had gone unnoticed was the woman disappearing out in the coverall suit along with Macleod. She'd then gone into the back of the forensic wagon, where she'd been changed into other clothes. Her face covered, she'd joined Macleod in a car to where no one except Macleod knew.

Hope had told Macleod not to tell Laura where she was going. Meanwhile, she was orchestrating the circus that was going on. It had to be played straight. Their killer could be watching. Also, there could have been an inside contact. Somebody paid to advise what had happened afterwards to make sure that Laura was dead.

Hope watched as the body bag was carried out of the room and then down the stairs and out to the one of the forensic wagons outside. Hope wasn't sure how Jona had done it but it looked like any of other body bags she'd seen. Jona was her usual self. Quiet, efficient, but sombre. Hope made sure she looked downcast the whole time.

'I'll get into the body and have a look, but there's not much to say. Two holes to the head,' said Jona. 'Dead. I'll get into the room up above, see if we can make anything of it. See if we can find something to find the killer.'

'We haven't found anything yet,' said Hope. 'We can't match her face, anywhere. If she's a contract killer, she's a good one, because she stays right off the radar. She's maybe never been caught.'

'There's big money involved, isn't there?'

Hope agreed and left Jona to go about her business. Hope picked up the phone and sent a message to Macleod which simply said, 'Complete at my end.'

A reply came back, saying, 'We're home.'

The first part of the shenanigans was over. They had got Laura to safety, but now they had to make sure that they picked up the killer.

She texted Perry advising him that everything was done and that the capture team would be along soon. They didn't wish to move until they'd got Laura safe, not wanting to give a warning. Hope was worried there was somebody inside the building, but now that Laura was safe, they could make their play for the killer, albeit one that wasn't guaranteed.

She picked up the phone and contacted a strike team leader, who she'd organised a few hours before. They were waiting a few miles away, and would now drive towards Perry's location, ready to seek out the woman. Cunningham would meet them, stay at a distance and report back on what was happening. Perry sat in the car beside Susan Cunningham, waiting for the strike team to arrive.

'You haven't had a cigarette for at least twenty minutes,' said

Susan.

'That really helps,' said Perry. 'If there's one thing that doesn't bring to mind needing a cigarette, it's being told that you haven't had one.'

'Sorry. I was just going to say I was impressed.'

'It's not impressive. I can actually go without them for an hour or two—when I need to.'

'Do you know what would bother me, though? The way they stink your clothes.'

'You can't smell them,' said Perry. 'It's like your nose doesn't smell anything after a while. You wonder if you've still got your perfume on.'

'Perfume?' said Susan.

Blast, thought Perry. *Something else to like about her.* He looked in the rearview mirror and saw a van pulling up. A man got out of it, dressed in fatigues, and got into the rear of Perry's car.

'She still there?'

'Yes,' replied Susan.

'We'll go. Stay clear here. Advise me if anything happens outside the perimeter that I need to be aware of.'

'Will do,' said Perry, taking an earpiece and a small mic off the man. 'Checking five, four, three, two, one.'

'I hear you loud and clear,' said the man. 'Just stay back. We'll sort this for you.' Perry nodded and watched as the van disappeared off again.

'I'll go in a bit closer,' said Susan. 'You hang back out here, okay?'

'I will do,' said Perry. 'Take care of yourself in there. Do nothing heroic. Those guys are trained for it. You're not. No heroics.'

'Can't let them have all the fun.'

'Seriously, Susan. No heroics. Contract killer. Don't do heroics around a contract killer. They can take you down before you've even known it.'

Perry watched Susan disappear off into the grounds of the hotel. Well, she'd stop short since she wasn't daft. But Perry knew the adrenaline that came in when you were close to finding someone, and if it went wrong, Susan would feel the need to step in. This was on the team that was going to get her. The strike team were the ones under examination now. Not Perry, not Susan.

They'd tailed her; they'd found her; they'd prevented a murder. It was all good. Macleod couldn't complain. Perry sat in the car. He'd need to move. If anybody came, he shouldn't be sitting here. He started the engine and drove approximately a quarter of a mile down the road. In his rear-view mirror, he could still see the entrance to the property. So he was happy he'd be able to pick out anyone arriving. In his earpiece, he could hear the strike team beginning to move.

Perry looked around him from his side of the road. On the other side, parked up beside a large yellow skip, was a car. The skip had been parked in the lay-by. The car too. Perry looked around him. Why would someone stop here? There were no paths to follow, no particular bit of wood to enter. The lay-by was almost out of place. But it had a view to the other side Perry thought was passable. There were so many views around here; that was the problem. He was spoiled for choice.

Perry heard the first moves, the strike team spreading out. There were code words but everything, as far as he could tell, was going smoothly. He looked around again. The car was bugging him.

There was a go command in Perry's ear, and he wondered about the strike team all thundering in, guns at the ready, trying to find their target. He gave a yawn, rolled down the window, and lit up a cigarette. Could he give them up for her, he thought, and then he chided himself. Susan wasn't about giving stuff up for. Susan wasn't anything but a colleague. Maybe a friend. She was darn likeable, though.

Perry decided that sitting around was getting to him, so he stretched, and he looked over at the car again. It was a hire car. He wondered when it had been hired and why would you leave it in the lay-by. Suddenly, in his ear, a loud noise was ringing. It sounded like a fire alarm. His phone rang. He saw it was Susan and answered it.

'Perry, the fire alarm's gone off. The strike team went in and the fire alarm went off. There's people running everywhere. It's chaos.'

Something sparked in Perry's mind. 'Susan, I think they're doing this to get away. They're running. It's not a real fire alarm. It's just creating the chaos to get out. I'm stuck here beside a car that shouldn't be here.'

'Where?' asked Susan.

'About a quarter of a mile down.'

'Well, don't tell me. You told me to stay put. Tell the strike team.'

In Perry's ear, the strike team were on the move, running here, there and everywhere. He could hear them calling out, asking if anyone could see the woman.

'Strike team, this is DC Perry.'

There were a few more instructions. And then, 'Perry, go!'

'I think there's a car down the road. I think it's the escape car. They're going to be coming here.'

'Negative, negative. In the building still. We have seen no one come out that matches target's description.'

Perry sat for a minute. He didn't want to talk on the mic too much because there seem to be so many instructions passing from the strike team to each other. It must have been bedlam in there. Perry sat in the car, looking around him, but there were no other cars on the road.

He turned and looked at the car again. A hire car. Why a hire car here? It wasn't right. Then he saw a figure approaching the car. It was coming from across the field, dressed in jeans and a large jumper. The figure had a hat on as well, and what looked like a beard and moustache.

Perry must have got it wrong. *Just some tourist out. Just somebody out for what*, thought Perry. *The alarm's gone off. Out they come. We can't find them. And a hire car? There was a man coming towards the hire car, walking out of a field.*

Perry watched the man get into the car. He couldn't quite convince himself completely, could he? He couldn't say that this was definitely wrong. It was more of a hunch. More of a thought. He heard the other car start up.

Screw it, thought Perry. *Do it and be damned.'*

He turned on the engine of his own car, quickly put the accelerator down and dropped the handbrake. His car lurched across the road and he crashed it into the side of the car parked beside the skip. The car bounced against the skip, Perry's own car resting alongside it. Quickly, Perry opened his own car door and flung himself out of it. He was down low and crawling across the road now. He began rolling, thinking he wasn't quick enough. When he reached the other side, he dropped into a ditch and felt a splash around him. It wasn't deep, but his whole back was soaking.

Quickly, he raised the phone up above the ditch and took a photograph, before bringing it down and looked at what was going on. The person inside the car seemed to be desperate to get out. But Perry had done a good job of it. He'd slammed his car up tight against theirs.

'Strike team, Perry.'

'What is it?' said the strike commander, and then reluctantly, 'Go!'

'I have trapped the suspect in a car approximately a quarter of a mile east, down the road from the entrance to the hotel. Request backup. I say again, trapped in a car but may get out soon. I may be compromised as well.'

'Get clear,' said the strike commander. 'On our way. Quickly.'

Perry tried to stand up. He looked and saw the figure in the car struggling. Perry hauled himself out of the ditch and walked along the road back towards where the strike team would be coming. He kept looking around him. She was getting out now, wasn't she? She was definitely getting out.

The rear window of her car was being hit by something. Did she have a gun? Perry didn't know. The windscreen suddenly cracked. He heard it and he ran for all he was worth. He was shouted after and he heard the glass shatter completely.

She'd be getting out. She'd be . . .

Perry saw a van approaching, hurtling towards him. He waved his hands frantically, recognising it for what it was, the strike team. But they raced right past him, the van coming to a screeching halt. Perry turned round and looked back.

The team was spreading out. In his earpiece, he heard the instructions. There was a cry from the strike leader, asking for hands to be held up, asking for someone to go down on their knees. There were more commands, and then Perry heard the word 'secured.' Only then did he stop walking away. He turned, and started to walk back. Behind him, Susan was running down the road.

'Are you okay?' she asked.

'Fine.'

'Look at you. You're soaked. Absolutely drenched. What did you do?'

'I ran the car into her car.'

Then Perry heard, in his earpiece, 'male apprehended.' He continued walking quickly back, heading towards the car he'd smashed into. As he approached, some of the team turned to him, guns raised, but then put them back down when they realised who it was.

'You said we were looking for a female. The descriptions we have are female.'

'Have you checked? Is she unarmed?'

'He's unarmed,' said the strike commander. Perry marched up and pulled off the hat the person was wearing. He grabbed the beard, yanking at it, and there was an almighty rip and a cry to the air.

'You haven't got a he. You've got a she. She's disguised. Somebody knew you guys were coming. I need to phone Hope. I need to tell her.'

As he picked up the phone, he felt a tap on the shoulder. Susan looked at him. 'No heroics, you said. What's this?' Perry looked over at the captured contract killer. His hands were shaking.

'I'd like a cigarette.'

Chapter 15

Hope punched the air. They'd got her. They'd actually got her. She jumped in her car, racing round to the hotel. She needed to congratulate the strike team. As she approached, she saw that the road was closed off. She stopped, took out her warrant card and was waved through.

'Perry. Brilliant,' she said, getting out of the car. She walked right past him and over to the strike commander. 'Good job, sir,' she said. 'Well done. Delighted.'

'Lucky, or rather, one of your team did a rather fine job.'

'What do you mean?' asked Hope.

'Well, we made the strike at the hotel where she was staying. She set off the fire alarm, escaped disguised as a man, but your man over there spotted it. He rammed his car into hers to stop her from getting away.'

'Well, well done, anyway. I assume you picked her up afterwards,' said Hope.

'Yes, indeed.'

'Right. Take her back to the local station and lock up. Stay on her. I don't want you guys disappearing. We need to make sure she's secured properly.'

'We won't leave until you come, and are happy.'

Hope watched him take the woman, put her in the van, which then drove off. Perry was sitting at the side of the road with Susan beside him. Hope approached him.

'Are you all right?' asked Hope.

'I'm fine,' said Perry.

'You should get checked over, anyway.' She stood and looked at him. It was a long way down to Perry on the ground, from Hope's height. She saw Susan smiling.

'What were you thinking?' asked Hope.

'Contract killer,' said Perry. 'No, it wasn't. It was something more than that, wasn't it? It was—it was getting your contract killer. I saw the opportunity. I did it.'

'Perry, she could have been sitting in that car with a gun!' spat Hope.

'Unlikely,' said Perry. 'I did factor that in.'

'He's just been a hero,' said Susan. 'She'd have been gone. She'd have been out of here. We'd have been—'

'That's enough Constable. I'm talking to Constable Perry. A contract killer. I brought in a strike team. You were to hang back.'

'I was hanging back. We were doing it right, and I called it and I said to the strike team she's coming here and they didn't come.'

'And what was your evidence?'

'We had the car on this lay-by beside a skip. Why would you be parked here? That was a getaway. That was a getaway parked there. Just in case. She's seen them coming. She set the fire alarm off. This was her go-to. This was her get out, and I saw it. I called it, and they didn't come.'

'And I could have had a dead officer in my hands. Damn it, Perry,' said Hope. 'No charging around. No heroics. We were up against a trained killer. We haven't got the ability to apprehend her safely. That's why we brought in a strike team. We're investigators. We're not people who just smash and grab.'

'If she'd have gone, if she'd have found out about Laura, she'd have come back for her,' said Perry very matter-of-factly.

'Get yourself cleaned up. I'll talk to you again. Perry, I'm not happy. Okay? And Macleod wouldn't see it any other way.'

'Yes, he would. You guys charge in. He's not averse to being beyond the book, especially when it comes to apprehending someone. You risk your lives all the time. It's no big deal.'

'It's a bloody big deal, Perry. I only just got you on the team. I said no heroics.'

He stood up. Turned to face her. 'Yes, Inspector.' He strode off.

'Where are you going?' asked Hope.

'Somewhere where I can get changed. Get back to my digs.'

'Now, you made this mess. Make sure it's all cleared up.'

Hope saw Susan's face, a thunderous scowl across it, and wholly directed at Hope.

'And I don't need you looking at me like that, Cunningham,' she said. 'I've said what I think about this. I am over the moon that we have her. But I'm not over the moon how it happened. I'll talk to the strike team as well. You called it and they weren't listening. That'll be a discussion too. In the meantime, let's get on with it.' Hope turned and went to walk away before looking back over her shoulder.

'I'll get a constable to drop one of the other cars down for you. Get this all cleared up, though.'

Hope arrived at the local station where the contract killer was sitting in an interview room. The strike team were guarding her, guns still, ready to be deployed. Hope came in and started the recording device and sat down with the strike team leader. The next thirty minutes were the most annoying of her recent days. Hope tried to ask every question going, but the woman wasn't for speaking. She got no name from her. When she stepped outside, she could see the strike team leader was annoyed, too.

'Remain here with her.'

'I don't think she'll speak,' he said.

'Do you think?' said Hope. 'We need to tie her comprehensively to Donal's murder. However, we have her for the attempted murder of our other woman. I might need to go at this differently. But before I do, my officer told you what was happening. My officer called it and you never reacted to it.'

'In my defence,' said the strike team leader, 'it was all kind of busy. It was chaos out there. We're trying to scan faces for a woman who all we've got is a sketch of, while everybody is running around. Should I have paid more attention to him? Maybe. But that's a hard call.'

'You didn't make him react the way he did. I have just taken him apart for doing that. But I don't think you made the right call.'

'Looking back's the easy bit. These captures are never easy,' said the strike team leader.

'I know,' said Hope, 'but it's the bit we need to get right. I'll make a note of it in my report, that's it. Thank you for your assistance. At least you got there and kept him alive. She'd have killed him.'

'Without a doubt,' said the strike team leader. 'I'll monitor her here until you get back to me.'

Hope rounded up the custody sergeant and went off to talk

to the suppliers of the women. The four men were in separate cells and Hope was accompanied by a constable as she went into the first cell.

'I've just picked up a contract killer. She was in amongst your women. She killed Donal Diamond, and she just tried to kill one of the other women. As I see it, you're heavily implicated in this since she was one of the women you supplied.'

Hope didn't believe that for a minute, but she thought it might get him talking.

'She's not one of ours. We have no killers. All the women are trafficked. All the women, we bring from Europe. One from Asia, but she came in through Europe. She was the one who ran away. We don't do this. Yeah? We're not into murder.'

'You admit to the trafficking, then.'

'Yes, but not murder. Nothing to do with us.'

'Then who is she?'

'How do I bloody know? She's not with us. I supply women. Sexy women. Yeah? The women, they get food, clothing. They know this if they do their job.'

'And if they don't?'

'We teach them to do their job if they don't.' Hope didn't like the sound of that.

'When you arrived, you came with twenty women, yes?'

'Yes, we have twenty. Ten from one place, ten from another. We don't meet up beforehand. The four of us. There's a two and a two, yes? The women stayed in the caravan.'

'And you're sure this woman wasn't amongst them?' Hope you pulled a picture of the contract killer.

'No, we go through. We vet the women.'

'What does that mean,' said Hope.

'We see what they're like, yes? We check them. Make sure

they can perform.'

Hope was nearly sick to her stomach. She wanted to walk up and plant one right in the man's face. But it was more important to find out what was going on.

'Who contacted you for the women?'

'Mr Diamond.'

'How did he pay?'

'He paid in cash when we met him.'

'He paid you in cash. Where is that cash?' The man went silent. 'I asked you where that cash is.'

Again, the man said nothing. Hope wondered, was he telling the truth, or was he covering up something else?

'We left the women on the premises. We left them there for Mr Diamond to have his time with them. And then we would come back in three days. But no, he dies. You people are there. I can't get near them to get them away. Then you lift us. And your man, he assaulted me.'

'Please,' said Hope, 'you're holding a woman naked amongst four of you. The amount of stuff we can throw at you is ridiculous. Don't even begin. Turn round and have a think again.'

Hope walked out and met the strike team leader. 'Any better,' he said.

'No,' said Hope. 'No!'

She walked out of the corridor into the station proper, got into her car, and drove back to the Strontian base they'd set up. She saw Cunningham's car there. When she entered, Cunningham and Perry were sitting behind their desks.

'The killer's not talking,' said Hope, 'not saying a word. I spoke to our four traffickers—well, one of them. He says that they got paid by Donal, and dropped the women off the day of the murder—well, the day before the morning murder. And then they got scared. The women were meant to be there for three days. The women were meant to—'

'He's lying,' said Perry. 'It makes no sense.'

'It doesn't, does it?' said Hope. She picked up the phone and called Macleod.

'Yes,' said Macleod. Hope could hear a noise of a car driving along in the background.

'Are you still with her?'

'No. I'll be back with you shortly.'

'We've got the killer. After some heroics by Perry.'

'Heroics,' said Macleod.

'Yes, Perry fancied himself as a driver. Crashed into the other car. He put himself at risk. I'm not happy.'

'I'll talk to you when I'm back,' said Macleod, 'but he's your man. You make the rules.'

'My problem is, Seoras, that I have no idea who hired this killer.'

'You've still got Ross out there though, haven't you?' asked Macleod.

'He needs to come up with some solutions. I can't be looking at sixty different siblings. Sixty different claimants.'

'Well,' said Macleod, 'if that's the case, that's the case. I'm sure we'll be able to eliminate them. I mean, some of them might be half a world away. Some of them couldn't afford the killer.'

'Except you could afford the killer if the money was promised afterwards.'

'What sort of contract killer doesn't get some of it up front, though?' asked Macleod. 'She was top dog in this world.'

'I guess it depends on the sum of money,' said Hope.

'Well, that's a thought,' said Macleod. 'What are you going to do?'

'I'm going to talk to Ross. He better have come up with something. It's time for the sergeant to pull his weight.'

Chapter 16

Ross was sitting in front of his laptop, currently trawling through detail surrounding the name Fergus Finnegan. Thankfully, it wasn't that difficult a name to find, although Ross thought it was highly popular for a fictional name. It might not have been what many parents would have called their children. Alas, one couple did.

He searched through Edinburgh records, working his way out from the city centre to see if he could find anywhere with some Finnegans. He found a couple of names that matched, but could trace them to birth records that show that they weren't orphans. But then he found a man who appeared to be the Fergus Finnegan he was looking for. He was located on a housing estate outside of Edinburgh, and Ross decided a visit was in the best interest of the investigation.

As Ross arrived at the estate that Fergus Finnegan lived on, he noted it was one of the more rundown ones. *It is probably cheap to live here*, Ross thought. Or at least, as cheap as Edinburgh ever got. Scottish cities, and Ross supposed like many cities, were a real mix of high-class housing and urban deprivation. He was closer to the urban deprivation now. As he turned the corner, he saw an upturned shopping trolley with some smashed glass between the houses. Two doors were boarded up and a few windows. When Ross parked his car, he locked it.

Ross stepped out onto the pavement and walked up a small driveway to a semi-detached house. The driveway had weeds growing through it. The garden looked completely unkempt, and Ross stared down at his feet.

He kept his shoes in pristine condition. He might have to give them a brush when he got back to his accommodation. Ross arrived at the front door and searched for a doorbell—it didn't seem to exist—and he couldn't find a knocker, either. Instead, he rapped the door with his hand, waiting to see if he'd get any response.

At first there was nothing, so he rapped on the door again. Once more, nothing. Ross walked across to the large window, presumably belonging to the living room of the house. He looked in and saw a man sitting on the sofa. He was in a dressing gown and looked like he'd seen better days. Ross rapped the window because the man wasn't looking over at him. The man looked and then just shook his head.

Ross wondered how to play this and then decided to be extremely formal. He reached inside his jacket, pulled out his warrant card and badge and held it up to the window. The man reluctantly got to his feet, and it took a good minute and a half before he arrived at the front door. He pulled it open. Ross could smell the alcohol on his breath.

'Hello, my name's Detective Sergeant Alan Ross. I'm looking to speak to Fergus Finnegan. Are you he?'

'I didn't do nothing. That fight started all on its own.'

'I'm not here to talk about the fight, sir. Would you mind if I come inside?'

'What are you here for, then?' asked the man. Ross noted he was hanging on to the door more than standing beside it.

'I'd like to talk about your brother.'

'Brother?'

'Yes, Donal Finnegan.'

'Why do you want to talk about Donal? Are you sure you're the cops? Are you a journalist?'

'I take it you've heard that—'

'Of course, I've bloody heard. It's all over the news. Bloody Donal. Set fire to his own bloody building. Arsehole!'

'Would you mind if I came inside and talked to you about him?'

'Yeah, I would, actually,' said Fergus. 'I damn well would. I don't want to talk about him. A wee gobshite. Do you know how long ago I left him? Do you know how long ago? And you know what happened? He made his money, and did he ever come and look after his family? Did he hell! He didn't even come to Rosheen's funeral. A hit and run. I had a hit and run to deal with and he didn't even turn up because he was off with that bloody guitar. That was Rosheen. Rosheen used to look after him in that orphanage. Rosheen was . . . Rosheen was the best. What do I get? A crappy place like this.'

'Have you been here the last couple of weeks?' Ross asked.

'Yeah. I haven't been out of Edinburgh in, oh, two years?'

'Can you prove it?'

'Do I need to prove it?'

'We believe that there is suspicion around the death of your brother.'

'Well, don't bloody point the finger at me. Anyway, I heard he died with twenty naked women around him. Didn't see him bringing them down here for me. I just get the sodding booze. And it's the cheap stuff. Not even anything good. He'd have been knocking back fifty-year-old whisky.'

Ross wasn't sure if fifty-year-old whisky existed. That was beside the point. Clearly, the man was agitated.

'Well, if you don't mind, sir, I would like to—'

'I bloody well mind. Okay? I do. If you don't mind, I'm going to just go back in there and sit and watch the telly.'

'What's on?' asked Ross.

'How the hell should I know? It just sits there, doesn't it? It's just a telly. Anyway, you can piss off, copper. Really, you can. I'm sick of them. Sick of them. All you ever do is come round and take this off us, take that off us.'

'What did we take off you?' asked Ross.

'You didn't take it off him, did you? I heard Donal was smacked out of his head. Smacked out of his head with naked women and booze and burnt himself alive. I don't know why you're spending the time on him. He never spent the time on anybody else. Wasting your time looking for somebody to kill him. Killed himself, anyway.'

'Are you all right, John? Who's that with you?'

Ross turned to see a Salvation Army worker on the street. He was dressed in a jacket with the church's logo on one side, smart, black trousers underneath.

'It's the bastard police. Talking about Donal's death.'

'Tragic,' said the worker.

'He won't piss off, though. Keep telling him they should sod off. I don't need to talk to him. I don't need to know anything about my brother. Went and killed himself, didn't he? I'm getting fed up with this. Do you know what? I've got a good mind to take one of those bottles in—'

'We don't want to be doing that now, do we? John!'

Ross was wondering why the man was calling him John. But he let the worker approach.

'Why don't I take you inside,' said the worker. 'Probably best for all of us. We don't want this policeman being subject to one of your lashings out, eh? It got you in trouble last time, didn't it?'

'It wasn't my fault. Took my booze, didn't he?'

'We're not going to talk about fault, are we? Let's just get inside. Yeah? Get inside and we'll calm down a bit. Is that okay for you, officer?' said the man.

Ross nodded, turned, walked back down the driveway, and sat in his car. He could see through the large window in the semi-detached house that the worker had taken Fergus back through to the living room and deposited him on a sofa. He then brought a cup of tea, but in between swigs of tea, Fergus was lifting a whisky bottle to his mouth. From what Ross could see, it certainly wasn't a fifty-year-old bottle. It was more like the stuff you lifted off the cheap counter at the supermarket.

Ross watched as the worker sat down with Fergus and was talking to him, seemingly gently. After about half an hour, he stood up, left the room, and came back with a blanket, wrapping it around Fergus. It took a while to help clear the room up, and Ross noted the worker going outside to drop glass bottles into a bin. They sorted some rubbish as well. Having done that, the worker exited the house and was making his way down the driveway, when Ross stepped out of the car.

'Can I have a word?' said Ross.

'Sure,' said the man, 'but probably best that I don t get in the car with you. I think John's asleep. But if he isn't, I don't want him to think that we're in cahoots. Not that I've anything against the police, and I'm sure you're here for an excellent reason.'

'I'll meet you round the corner,' said Ross.

Ross returned to the car, waited until the man had turned around the corner and then drove to park beside him. The man got into the passenger side and Ross pulled out his warrant card.

'DS Alan Ross. I don't know if you've heard, but Donal Diamond died. Did you know? He was Fergus's brother.'

'Oh, I'm well aware,' said the man. 'Well aware.'

'I'd like to talk a bit about Fergus. About how he is.'

'I don't mean to be funny, but as a Salvation Army worker, are you telling me to tell you or am I being asked if I want to talk about him?'

'Why?' said Ross. 'Is there something incriminating?'

'No. I have confidences with him. Like you would with anyone. I don't want to bring up his life. I stepped in there because Fergus, at times, can get violent. Kicks off. But I don't want to say any more.'

'What's your name?' asked Ross.

'John,' said the worker. 'Ironic, isn't it? I'm John. John Maloney.'

'I noticed you were calling Fergus John.'

'It's just a thing he's got in his head since his brother died. Didn't want to be identified with, and was going on about, not wanting that past. He needed a bright new future. Needs a lot more than a new future. He needs proper counselling. He needs to get off the drink and the drugs.'

'He takes drugs, too.'

'Probably said too much,' said John.

'I could make this official,' said Ross. 'You see, I'm investigating the murder of Donal Diamond.'

'Didn't say on the radio that it was murder.'

'They probably reported it as suspicious. We are looking into it. There was initial talk of suicide but no, I'm looking into the murder. So I need to understand about his brother. I need to understand where he was. And anyone who can help me with that, I will bring in for a conversation. If he's innocent, then it's best we know all the facts about him and exonerate him quickly.'

'I don't believe it about John. Sorry, Fergus, it gets confusing after a while, doesn't it?'

Ross shrugged his shoulders. 'Are you going to talk to me? Or do I need to make this formal?'

'Do you need to talk to me right now? I'm actually on my way to run an open house morning. I'll be done about lunchtime. Maybe we could speak then, somewhere not on the estate. Forgive me, you scream policeman. It's not that I have any problems with you or what you do, and at times we work closely with you. But some people here wouldn't talk to me if they saw me talking openly to you. And I want to put them at the forefront.'

'Fair enough,' said Ross. 'I'll pick you up then.'

'Don't,' said the man. 'When I say they wouldn't be happy, they really wouldn't be happy. I've got a car at the centre. Do you know the garden centre, out towards the ring road there?'

'Passed it on the way in. About two, three miles away?'

'Most of the people here wouldn't get anywhere near it. We'll go there.'

'Okay,' said Ross. 'I have to warn you that if you say something that I need, I'll have to take a full statement.'

'I've no problems doing that,' said the man. 'You understand this is just so the work can continue with no hassle.'

Ross smiled and let the man get out of the car.

Ross drove off to the garden centre, sat down with his laptop and a coffee, and started looking back through the records. He had found Fergus Finnegan and needed to know exactly what sort of person he was. Ross picked up his messages and found that Hope had left him a message asking him to concentrate on who had hired the contract killer.

Ross sighed. Things just weren't the same. These days, he didn't know what it was about. He was there today and all he could feel was annoyance at this poor man. All he wanted to do was get to the truth and get on with it and get home. He sat back, sipping coffee.

Ross realised that of all the people on the team, he was the one struggling the most. Perry had come into a new team and made a complete mess of introducing himself, and yet he seemed to be quite happy at the moment. He was engaging Susan and had hit the ground running.

Hope was taking command and Clarissa had gone off finding her own team to work with, taking Patterson with her. Ross wasn't sure what he was doing at the moment despite his step up to sergeant. Things just didn't feel right. It wasn't the same without the boss being the boss. He wished for the days of Macleod back. And yet he didn't quite know why.

Chapter 17

Hope sat at the makeshift desk in Strontian, looking at the email that Ross had sent her. He had advised her that morning he was working to find someone closer to Fergus Finnegan, the brother of Donal, and that he was getting close to understanding the man. He also had sent through the large number of claimants to Donal's fortune.

Hope looked through them, shaking her head. It would take ages to work through all these people. She'd have to divide them up—likely, less likely, extremely unlikely—then get a task force on it. She wondered if anyone had come after him, though, made a play asking Donal for money. The person who might know would be Evangeline. After all, she'd lived with Donal. He clearly had other partners when she was about. And maybe she would know who the more vehement ones were.

It would be worth a shot anyway, because at the moment, Hope was struggling to narrow down the extensive list that Ross had given her. It being a contract killer, the person who actually organised Donal's death could have been anywhere at that time. But at least she had the killer in custody, thanks to Perry.

That'd had been a turn up for the books. But it was a good

one. Hope decided to go to Evangeline and jumped in her car and drove the short distance to the house, where she knocked on the door. She found Evangeline dressed in a pair of Lycra shorts and a crop top.

'Oh, Inspector, isn't it? Sorry, I'm just in the back doing my workout for today. Well, I was actually, on the bike. Have you got one of these things? You can join in with everyone around the country.'

'No,' said Hope. 'I don't really have the time.'

'Well, you have to make time for your health, don't you?' said Evangeline.

'Can I come in?' asked Hope.

'Of course, you can,' said Evangeline. 'I'm well to the rear of the house.'

Evangeline took Hope through to a small gym room where a stationary bike had a screen in front of it. Hope could see several other riders on that screen.

'Simulated. It's nice, you know,' said Evangeline. 'I go on this and nobody knows who I am. But they talk to me using my nickname. Nobody knows who I was married to.'

'Do you find it difficult being independent?'

'Of course, I do. I'm always going to be Donal's ex. At least the press hasn't got in. They're a pain. I mean, they know where I am. They came around, but I pretended I wasn't here. But they'll be back.'

'They sure will,' said Hope. 'But can I ask you something?'

'You're a detective,' said Evangeline. 'I was kind of expecting you'd get round to it.'

Hope smiled. 'There's numerous claimants for Donal's fortune.'

'Indeed,' said Evangeline.

'Well, I think you told me before that you and Donal had trouble. And he had other partners.'

'He was like a nymphomaniac, the number of partners he had,' said Evangeline. 'You feel betrayed.' Evangeline stopped pedalling the bike she was on, stepped off it and mopped herself down with a towel. 'Look at yourself,' said Evangeline, 'what are you, in your thirties, mid-thirties maybe? You're a good-looking woman, if you don't mind me saying so, Inspector. What are you, six-foot, red hair? Men like red hair, different. You're in good shape; maybe you've got a partner. Oh, you do!'

'How did you know?'

'Your mouth inflected slightly when I said it—almost an involuntary smile. That's good. I'm happy for you. But imagine if he started to just, well, if you use the coarse term, shag most women around him.'

Hope replied, 'I wouldn't be thrilled.'

'No, and it is a betrayal. Stepping outside of what we promised to each other is a betrayal. If he had said to me, "I'm going to be more promiscuous; I'm going to be with these women, and I'd agreed to it," It would have been okay. Your marriage becomes more of a contractual binding than the thing of love. The thing is, I loved Donal. But when he did that, well, suddenly I'm a woman who's struggling. What got me was Donal doing it after Tee-Tee was born.'

'What about the money you got in the separation?' Hope asked. 'Is it enough?'

'It has to be,' said Evangeline. 'I will not benefit any more from Donal.'

'What settlement did he give you, if you don't mind me asking?'

135

'I don't mind you asking, but it is not to be made common knowledge. I got five million from Donal and bought this rather delightful house with it. There's a yearly stipend that comes out of the savings. I put some money out to parts of my family. We did okay from it. I'm more than comfortable and can go on holiday several times a year. I don't have to work. There's also a small nest egg for Tee-Tee.'

'But now that he's dead, you'll get more money, won't you?'

'No,' said Evangeline. 'There's a clause in our settlement that says that I cannot be part of the inheritance if he died. I thought five million was fair enough. I didn't want to fleece him or destroy him. All I wanted was out.'

'But he must have done some damage to you—sleeping with all those women.'

'Well, yes, he did damage me.'

'Enough to want him dead?' asked Hope.

'If I were to kill Donal, it would be a little unfair.'

'Unfair?' queried Hope, thinking that was an unusual term. 'Why unfair?'

'Because I was the first one to be unfaithful, at least the first one who owned up to it. Donal was spending so much time away. I was frustrated. I was lonely. All the usual stuff. I met a man. And I, well, yeah, we did it. It wasn't anything earth-shattering. It wasn't anything dynamic. I didn't come away from it suddenly feeling like a more fulfilled woman. I probably came away from it feeling quite shabby.'

'So you feel, what, this offset all his women?'

'Of course it doesn't offset them all,' said Evangeline. 'But what it did was almost give him an excuse.'

'Forgive me, because I'm struggling with this,' said Hope. 'He's clearly a man who enjoys women. And you are a good-looking woman.'

'Yes, but he had a thing for the younger women as well, though.'

'I'm thinking,' said Hope, 'that if my partner did that to me, I would not just feel upset. I would feel anger. Strong enough anger to—'

'To want to kill them. You speak like a woman who's never been cheated on.'

Hope thought back. She never had, had she? She'd never had that done to her. There was one or two she'd maybe suspected, but it had never been proven.

'Does that make a difference?' Hope asked.

'Of course it makes a difference. We're all different, but you fall apart. You know, it's taken me a while to understand that I am what I am.'

'So what, you don't feel anger to him?'

'I love Donal. I don't feel anger, just pity. To go through all these women and not get any satisfaction, to be with that many conquests as he would have seen it and not be satisfied. He must well . . .'

'What is it you feel?'

'He was a decent man, underneath it all.'

'Forgive me,' said Hope. 'I'm really struggling to see that. Drink, drugs, groupies, split up from yourself and his child.'

'No,' said Evangeline. 'You don't understand. Tee-Tee was Donal's idea.'

'I really don't understand,' said Hope. 'Tee-Tee was Donal's idea.'

'Yeah,' said Evangeline, tears running down her face. 'I got pregnant from that one time. He could have got rid of me; he could have turned around and said goodbye. But he didn't.

137

Donal accepted me back in. He said, keep Tee-Tee and he supported Tee-Tee all the way until she was eighteen. He said he would do that.

'She's not his child. Tee-Tee is in his face as the memory of what his partner did to him. And yet he embraced her. Don't get me wrong, Inspector; he ended up a mess. And maybe I did part of that to him. Maybe he did a lot to himself. It could have been the music industry. Maybe it was the fact that none of them actually give a toss about him. But he tried. Tried to care for Tee-Tee and in his own way for me. I don't feel bitter about him. I feel sorry.'

'Forgive me again,' said Hope, 'for prying. How do you know Tee-Tee wasn't his? I assume at the time you were, what, not having sex?'

'No, we were having sex. The thing is that the reason we hadn't had kids up to that was because we couldn't. We got checked out. We went to see and Donal, well, Donal was sterile.'

Hope tried to process what she'd just heard. 'Sterile.'

'All these claimants, all these—'

'Let me understand this. My colleague has got about sixty so-called children of Donal. Illegitimate. Claims from women he bedded, or from their children, that they are Donal's offspring. And they're all going to come into this inheritance. And you're telling me that none of these claims are true. You're telling me that Donal's sterile?'

'Check his medical records. They are in there.'

Hope felt like she wanted a seat. This changed everything. Suddenly the numbers of people they were looking at were cut down.

'I don't know what arrangements Donal has put in place for

his death,' said Evangeline. 'All I know is that I won't be in them. Legally, I deserve nothing. I can't be in them. I've made my peace with him, financially, morally, spiritually. Does he do anything for Tee-Tee? I don't know. He didn't share that with me. I found it hard to be around him when he was that much of a mess. But that's because I loved him. Can you understand that, inspector?'

Hope nodded, but her mind was racing. 'Do you know if he ever saw much of his brother?'

'Donal rarely talked about them. I told you he was a good man. I don't understand what went on between them, or not, but Donal was caught up with the music. You need to process that. A lot of what Donal did bad in his life came out of this obsession with the fame, the fortune, and the music. Donal could play a guitar. Donal could sing. He was something else. But all the trappings that came with it, which they didn't protect him from, destroyed him and destroyed any thought of his family.

'He took it hard when Rosheen died. But rather than grieve with his family, he buried himself in his music; he buried himself into this other life. How his family saw that, I don't know. We didn't see them. He didn't take us to be with them, ever. I've never even met Fergus.'

'Thank you,' said Hope. 'I think you've just changed a lot of what I'm looking at.'

'If you want any more, of course, I'll speak to you again,' said Evangeline. 'Just try to keep the press away from me. I'd appreciate that.'

Hope nodded and walked out to her car. She sat inside for a moment, thinking about Donal, and the way things had gone wrong for him. About Evangeline, still loving him, although she was staying away from him. And then, for a moment, Hope felt suddenly insecure. She'd never had a problem with her looks. But then again, Evangeline didn't either. Donal had fallen away from her. Hope picked up the phone.

'It's John here. Hello? You there, Hope?'

'I just wanted to hear your voice,' she said.

'Okay,' said John. 'That's unusual. Everything okay in the case?'

'I'm fine now,' she said.

'Can I ask what's up?' said John.

'Just a little moment of doubt. But hearing your voice has stopped it from becoming anything. I'll try to call you this evening.'

'OK,' said John, clearly bemused. 'If you need me, I'm here,'

'I know you are,' said Hope.

'Thank you.' She closed the call before he could ask any more.

She thought about Macleod and what Macleod had once said to her. How everything got so messy at the start. Everything was so widespread. And you ground away at it until it suddenly got closer and closer and narrowed down. But it had just taken a massive jump to narrowing. Hope smiled and returned to Strontian.

Chapter 18

Ross sat at the table in the coffee shop of the garden centre awaiting John Maloney, the Salvation Army worker. He'd sent Hope a massive list of all the potential children of Donal Diamond. Ross was disgusted by it. How could you be so reckless with children?

He had to work so hard for him and Angus to get a child, to have their boy. They had to demonstrate how loving they were, how they could provide, how they could be a proper couple for him. And here was somebody, willy-nilly spreading his seed like anything and not giving two hoots about the children he created. Ross was angry.

Some people had questioned whether he had the right to look after a kid because of his relationship with Angus. Not normal, not natural. Well, as far as Ross saw it, he was doing a better job of bringing up his child than Donal Diamond did with any of the mass children he had helped conceive. True fatherhood belonged to Ross.

Ross looked up and saw John Maloney strolling in. He was still in a Salvation Army jacket and Ross intercepted him so he could buy the man a coffee. They sat down in what was a fairly busy coffee shop, but Ross had located a table in the far corner of the room and said, 'I want to talk about Fergus. Just give me an idea about him, what you know about him, where he's been, what he's done.'

'Fergus struggles in life,' said John. 'He is the proverbial tortured soul. He grew up in an orphanage and, well, from what I gather, it wasn't the best situation. They were well looked after, they were provided for, they were set up to achieve, but they didn't all do it. His sister's death hit Fergus hard. He often tells about Donal never coming to the funeral.'

'Do you know why that was?'

'I only know Fergus's side,' said John, 'and from his point of view, the guy just didn't care.'

'Is there a deep resentment in Fergus about that?'

'Deep, very deep. He doesn't like people talking about Donal. They find out they're brothers and they only want one of two things. They think Fergus has got a lot of cash, which he doesn't, because Donal's never given him anything, according to Fergus. But it's also the fame side. You go into a conversation where everything is about Donal. Fergus is the side piece. Never asked to be. He was just put there by everybody. Donal did nothing to make him front and centre, and I think the resentment kicks in from there. That's the major problem. Donal just did nothing for him.'

'He clearly struggles with addiction,' said Ross.

'He's got major problems—struggles with the drink. He takes drugs. I guess, in many ways, he's like his brother. Would he be addicted to the sex like the tabloids report Donal is? Maybe, but he doesn't have the money to fuel that lifestyle. He's barely got the money to fuel his alcohol or any drugs. He's not taking high-quality stuff. Not that any of it's any good for you.

'I've tried to encourage him off it. I've tried to get him proper help, and he slumps away from it all. But you keep going, you know? That's why I'm here. That's what I do. I'm meant to befriend those who are lost. I'm meant to befriend those who are not pretty. Those who have struggled in society. That's the role.'

'So, he receives nothing from Donal?'

'He says that, but I saw a bank statement once, and I know there was some money going in. The other thing I know is that the drink and drugs he does buy, there is no way he could afford it on his own. But the money that goes in isn't enough to lift him out of the circumstance.'

'What do you mean?' asked Ross.

'As far as I understand it,' said John, between munching on his roll, 'Donal Diamond was worth an absolute fortune. Millions. He's got a brother who's deep in addiction problems. Now, we're providing what services we can, the government, everybody else working on it. But, it would be unrealistic to say that our services are as good as the top people. The ones you can buy with serious money. The ones who can spend all their time and attention on you. Donal could have paid for that. But he didn't.

'Now, was that because he wouldn't impose that on Fergus? Is the money that he sent to Fergus just a way of appeasing his conscience? I don't know, but I do know that if it was, it certainly didn't help his relationship with Fergus.'

'What do you think Fergus spent the money on?'

'Booze, drugs. Fergus has got no forward vision. Fergus doesn't know what he wants to be. Donal, as I understand it from the papers, made it into being a big rock star. Then he fell apart. He had the drive that pushed all the things out. Maybe that's why they don't speak. But he had drive. Fergus hasn't. It's funny to have two siblings come up through the same roots and yet both end up being very different.'

'Very different until everything falls apart,' said Ross. 'Both drinking, drugs. Possibly Fergus would have turned to prostitutes as well if he'd had the money. Has he been in Edinburgh for quite a while? Has he taken any trips away?'

'He did, actually. He went on a trip abroad, but it certainly didn't seem to help.'

'Why would it help?' asked Ross.

'He said he was going to visit someone that would help.'

'Like a counsellor—medical people?'

'Gotta be careful when they say things. He's addicted to drugs. Some days he'll tell you he needs to get off them; other days, he'll tell you it's what's keeping him going. It varies every day. I don't know which it was. You can't always tell, and I'm not a professional in that sense.'

'But you know him well?'

'I've seen him most days.'

'So he definitely went on a trip abroad?'

'I guess so because he's still keeping the name Fergus Finnegan. This John thing's only happened recently, since the death of Donal. Don't ask me why.'

'So, his passport would have been as Fergus Finnegan. That's great. That's very useful. So, do you know if he ever saw any of Donal's family?'

'Don't think so. Don't remember him going up on a trip to see them. Don't remember anybody ever visiting. If I recall correctly, Donal has a child, and an estranged wife. Is that right?'

'Basically,' said Ross.

'I think Fergus is sad not to know his niece. Mentioned her

once or twice. Mentioned Evangeline by name, but I don't think he's ever met her. It's a hard thing talking to him at times. You're never sure what he knows and doesn't know, because sometimes he tells you and sometimes he doesn't. Sometimes we get an emotional rant. Getting him talking sensibly and seriously is difficult.'

Ross sat back down, lying into the chair behind him, thoughtfully. Was there any more he needed to know? The man had disappeared on a trip abroad. If he wasn't sure what it was for, he would have to check up on the passport records—see where he'd gone.

Someone had hired a contract killer. Maybe that had been done elsewhere. He was still checking up on who the killer was. If they knew that, they might find out their location. Where they operated out of.

One thing was bothering Ross, though. Did Fergus look like a man who could work a hit? He didn't have the money for a hit either. How did this all pan out? How did he hire someone?

Ross watched John Maloney, the Salvation Army worker, eating his roll, drinking his coffee. There was no reason to suspect the man was saying anything that he shouldn't have. His picture of Fergus was an intriguing one, but also one that said to Ross that the man wasn't a killer, or someone who could hire a killer. He seemed like a poor wretch. And yet, he had that trip away.

Ross looked around the garden centre, waiting for Maloney to finish his lunch before saying goodbye. As he did so, he saw somebody lingering on the edge of the coffee shop. Ross stood up as Maloney finished and when he looked over again, the man was gone. It was a man, thought Ross, because they were in a hoodie and the shoulders were definitely male. Big hands,

145

too.

Ross walked Maloney out through to the car park, shook hands with him on the doorstep and watched as Maloney headed off towards his car. Ross glanced around him and saw the same hooded figure looking over from the edge of the car park. Casually looking back to Maloney, Ross turned and then walked slowly over towards his car, which was towards the man in the hood. As he got to his car, Ross turned and sprinted, making a beeline for the man in the hood.

But he was quick. They turned, vaulted a stone wall behind them, and were off into fields by the time Ross got there. He jumped over the stone wall, landed in a field where his feet went from under him, and by the time he rolled back up, the hooded man was well gone into woods. Ross could not see where he'd gone.

Ross came back over the stone wall and looked for John Maloney, but he'd departed. So, he sat in his car. He called up border control and asked them to check on the movements of Fergus Finnegan. He passed on the address, date of birth, anything he had on the man. And then closed the call, waiting for them to call back.

Ross thought about John Maloney. He was there day in, day out, doing something good. Angus always said that Ross was doing something good. He was there protecting the public. Maybe he wanted to do something better.

After all, what did Ross do? He prodded into people's accounts. He nosed about in their affairs. Yes, he caught killers, but he looked at death all the time and he was kept away from home. Maybe he could do more if he could just, well, just get on with things and maybe help people out differently. He stopped, thinking, and then took out a pad of paper. He wrote three words on it.

'Am I happy?'

Was this a midlife crisis? Was this a job crisis? Why was everything different? What was the thing that was annoying him? Was it being a sergeant? He was out on his own here. Maybe that was preferable to working with Perry. But he wasn't working with Susan Cunningham. Hope had put Susan and Perry together. Ross was out on his own, checking through stuff.

Was that because he was more senior? Or had Hope just kept Perry and him apart? They weren't a good match. They really weren't. Susan Cunningham was. Ross always thought that she felt wholly professional with him. Ross didn't look at her as anything except a colleague. She had a reputation in the station, and he wondered if Hope was being wise, putting a man like Perry with her.

Ross realised it was half an hour later when the phone rang. He picked it up, sat and made notes while the man from border control advised him of Fergus Finnegan's trips.

'Oh, we got him all right. Tagged through. Landed at Seville in Spain.'

'How long did he stay?' asked Ross.

'Three days. Quick trip round.'

'Where did he fly from?'

'London Gatwick.'

'Thank you for that,' said Ross.

Why was Fergus Finnegan in Seville? Would he go back and ask him? Would the man defend himself? What would he say? And he wasn't a man who could afford a trip abroad, except with Donal's money. So why did he use it for that? Was it to do with drugs? Was it to do with any of his other vices?

Interesting, thought Ross. It was interesting. But truly his mind was elsewhere. 'Am I happy,' he thought. 'No. I want to go home.'

Chapter 19

Hope stepped inside the office at Strontian, chewing over in her mind what she'd just been told. Macleod was in the office, prepping himself for a press briefing.

'How's it getting on?' he asked.

'Well, I've just eliminated about sixty potential suspects.'

'Excellent,' said Macleod. 'How?'

'Donal's sterile.'

'And what? That definitely eliminates the potential for people to come and kill him? If they thought that his—'

'No, no, no. He's sterile. That's why he was quite happy sleeping around. It's one thing that he could tell women. Nobody is going to get his inheritance. If any of them had made an approach to him, he basically would just say he was sterile. It's telling me that these people have fabricated their stories.'

'Okay,' said Macleod. 'I don't think we should eliminate them, but put them on the back burner.'

'Of course,' said Hope. 'But we now need to go at those closest to him.'

'Namely who?'

'Well I've just been to Evangeline. I don't think it's her. She can't get any inheritance. She got given five million pounds in a separation settlement that stipulated that she would get nothing further. Evangeline cannot inherit, Seoras. She genuinely seems to have loved him but stayed away because it hurt so much. Tee-Tee's not Donal's because he's sterile. Donal was betrayed first by Evangeline, but Donal still kept Tee-Tee.'

'Okay, so there's definitely a connection between them, but he went and slept with all those other women.'

'She said she felt for him. It was more of an addiction, his inability to deal with the fame.'

'So where else do we go?'

'We've got to look at Tee-Tee as well. The other people we need to look at is his brother Fergus. Ross is on that at the moment. We need to look at Fags.'

'Larry Goodlad,' said Macleod. 'Fags is such a detrimental name, isn't it? I can't see him enjoying being called that.'

'You say that, but some people do. Anyway, I think I need to talk to Fags. At the very least he's going to understand these people. I can get a different view.'

'Ok, where's he staying?' asked Macleod.

'Well, he's still meant to be staying at the house. Except they've moved everyone out.'

Hope called Perry, who advised that Fags was now living in rented accommodation close to Strontian. Hope thanked him, asked Macleod if he wanted to come along for the interview.

'No, I'm back on to the press. I'm getting kind of bored with it. They just keep going on and on down the same lines. However, I have kept the notion of murder out of it. Suspicious death.'

'Good. Maybe it won't be too long before we're able to wrap

this. Susan's getting on to Interpol about our killer.'

'Good,' said Macleod. 'And you're okay with your team?'

'They seem to be doing alright, don't they?'

'Are you sure?'

Hope looked at him. 'Perry's doing okay,' she said. 'Been very helpful.'

'There's more than Perry in the team,' said Macleod. 'Make sure they're all okay.'

Hope nodded. She wanted to turn around and ask him what exactly he meant, but that would be giving in. Macleod obviously saw something. She was the DI now. She needed to see it first.

Hope gave him a wave, and walked out to her car, driving it round to the address that had been given to her by Perry. The house was a small cottage, and she walked up to the front door. She rapped on it loudly with the knocker. The grey stone walls of the cottage had been touched by a light flurry of rain and there were a few dabs on the windows. It seemed to take an awful long time for Fags to arrive, so she struck with the knocker again on the door. This time it was a lot louder.

'Just a moment!' came a voice. 'I'll be there in a second.' Hope noted that the windows, although they had rain on them, had the curtains drawn. She looked up and around. Every window had the curtains drawn. It was lunchtime. Blimey, he was seriously asleep all this time.

The door opened and Larry Goodlad stood in front of her with just a short dressing gown on.

'Oh, Inspector, it's you!'

'Expecting anyone else?'

'No, no, I just didn't know who it would be. But it's a delight to see you.'

'Can I come in? It'd be better than interviewing you on the doorstep dressed like that.'

'Oh, right, yes, maybe? That's a good idea.' Hope heard a door closing somewhere else in the house.

'Is that a door closing?'

'Yes,' said Fags. 'It's a door closing. It's just one of the women.'

'One of the women?' queried Hope.

'Yes,' said Fags. 'One of the women that serviced us. I got a call. She was offering services because she needed to make a bit of extra money.'

Hope thought that she needed to make a check on what was going on. After all, they were in protective custody.

'And so, she's just been here.'

'Earning some money.'

'Which woman was it?'

'I think she said she was Miranda. But I think that's a working name,' said Fags. 'I don't know what her real name is. But she was very enjoyable.' He gave a rather leery smile, which Hope didn't appreciate.

'Maybe if I come in, we can talk further. I want to talk to you about Donal and Evangeline but you could probably get changed before we do that.'

'Of course,' said Fags.

He escorted her into the living room where she sat down on the sofa while Larry Goodlad disappeared off to get changed. As she sat on the sofa, Hope looked around the room. There was definitely that musky smell in the air. She knew that someone had been here servicing Larry Goodlad. What a bizarre term, servicing. It was so distant. Hope felt a slight shudder.

John and she were intimate. It wasn't like this. She would

never service John. This world she was standing in was a strange one. She was struggling to understand it, a scenario she was not used to. Is this what your money bought you—debauchery on a plate?

Hope looked across the room and beside one chair was a bra sitting on the floor. Clearly, Miranda had left something behind. Larry Goodlad was still upstairs, so Hope wandered over with her phone and took a picture of the bra. It corroborated what he was saying after all, that a woman was here. She'd obviously fled quickly. Hope would talk to her later, and she'd also talk to Perry. What was going on?

Larry Goodlad bounced back into the room, now dressed in a pair of jeans and a t-shirt with a famous rock band blazoned across it. He hadn't touched his hair, nor had he washed. And he still smelt like someone who had been engaging in hot physical activity. It was an image that she didn't really want to see. Hope had seen a lot of these girls and she did think of a lot of them as girls. Not women. The idea of a man like this, paying to enjoy them, was not one she found attractive. The possibility they were not there by choice was deeply unpalatable.

'I have done nothing wrong, have I, by acquiring her services?'

'If she's come here willingly, but I'll check with her.'

'Please do,' said Larry. 'I didn't realise we were doing anything wrong. She offered, and I accepted.'

'They were trafficked women.'

'But, as I understand it, I heard you captured the men who were dealing them?'

'We have done,' said Hope. 'But I will check up on what you've said. I want to make sure you haven't coerced her.'

153

'God forbid,' said Larry Goodlad.

'Tell me something. I heard recently that Donal was sterile. Is that correct?' asked Hope.

'You guys really investigate, don't you? Yes, he was sterile. It's one of the things that he was not worked up about, as it meant he could be with women fully, shall we say.'

Hope didn't think it was anything like being with a woman fully. But if he meant to have full sex with them, well then, she could understand how it was easier with him being sterile.

'The one thing you need to understand, though, is that Evangeline hated Donal for his sterility. You know they tried to cover it up. That's not good, is it?'

'Tee-Tee's not his child, is she?' asked Hope.

'Well, I think she is. Because I think she was the happy accident before Donal lost his fertility.'

'And you put that down to what?'

'Drugs and the drink. I mean, Donal wasn't exactly the picture of perfect health. The things he did to his body, the abuse it suffered. Any body would react against that. And I think shutting down his reproductive function, so to speak, was maybe the payback. Quite ironic, though.'

'But do you think that Tee-Tee was a happy accident? You think that Tee-Tee—'

'Well, it happens, doesn't it? Especially in cases with, well, low counts.'

'Did he tell you this? Did he tell you anything about what his doctor had said?'

'He only spoke when he was drunk about it. So, what I know is what I heard. Was it accurate? Maybe. It certainly made sense from what I saw. And yeah, who can blame Evangeline? She took a lot from him. A lot of stuff that wasn't good and then he can't give her a kid.'

'But he did, according to your thoughts, he gave her Tee-Tee.'

'Well, I suspect he gave her Tee-Tee, but he clearly didn't give her any more.'

'So, all these people who claim that Donal's their father . . .'

'Highly unlikely,' said Larry Goodlad. 'Highly unlikely, but who knows? And hey, maybe they think they are and it's a good enough reason to kill somebody. Isn't it?'

'Possibly. What about his brother, Fergus, and Rosheen? Did he talk much to you about them?'

'Rosheen was a sore topic. He didn't talk about that. But he also had Fergus pestering him.'

'Pestering him?' queried Hope.

'Yes, for money. He always wanted money. I know he used to send money down to Fergus. Crazy. The guy did sod all for him. But the two of them didn't speak. You know that.'

'So I've heard. How long are you going to be here?' asked Hope.

'Well, I don't think I'm meant to leave while you're doing your investigation. Although, I guess I could head up to Edinburgh or somewhere. I'm reasonably local. As long as I tell you where I'm going?'

'Absolutely,' said Hope. 'But you need to keep in contact with us in case we have to ask you any further questions.'

'Well, maybe another couple of days.'

'Can I ask you something?' said Hope.

'I thought you were.'

Hope smiled. 'You give the impression that you sort of went along with this whole mass orgy thing, just because, well, you know, you were doing it for Donal. And then here I am, popping in and you're already with one of the women.'

'You get used to it, don't you,' said Larry. 'You get used to, well, that sensation? I guess you become a bit addicted to it as well. Donal wasn't the only one.'

Hope nodded. She was going to have to speak to Perry about the women—and especially about this Miranda. But she also needed to speak to Tee-Tee now. Maybe she would get Macleod to sit in.

Hope strode back to her car and drove towards Strontian. It was coming together. She was sure the picture was being painted. All she had to do now was to identify correctly what she was looking at. As she drove, she felt the thrill. The chase was on. The chase was almost there. Could she see it through? She thought so.

Chapter 20

Susan Cunningham was sitting waiting for the phone call from Interpol she'd been advised was coming. The contract killer had said nothing while she'd been held in the cells. And soon they would look to transfer her to a more secure holding facility. Susan had never been involved with a contract killing. It was certainly something different to the murders she'd experienced before.

They were now not looking for someone capable of murder, but someone capable of ordering it. They didn't have to do the deed. Instead, all they had to do was hire someone and have the money. That was proving to be a problem at the moment—money. There weren't that many people who could hire contract killers, and certainly not without withdrawing it out of a bank. They had checked the chief suspects. Nobody's account showed a large withdrawal of money, which made Susan suspect the killer might be someone as yet unknown. Or maybe it was one of these people who thought that Donal was their father or had given them a child.

Susan sat waiting patiently, as Perry footered about before bringing her a coffee. He stood off to one side, not in front of the laptop, telling Susan she'd be much better at this. Susan wondered if Perry had something in his past? Why did he not want to be on the screen? He was an awkward fellow in some ways, but she was warming to him in a way that the others didn't seem to.

The screen suddenly burst into life, and sitting opposite was an older man of around forty-five. He gave an enormous smile. Unfortunately, one of his teeth was missing, and Susan did her best not to stare, but said hello back.

'You're speaking to Detective Constable Susan Cunningham of Police Scotland.'

'My name is Juan Montoye and I'm an officer with Interpol. I was assigned to look at the photographs that you sent to us. We're quite surprised that you captured her. How did you do it?'

'We trailed her and one of our officers secured her inside a car by ramming it when she got in.'

'She's brutal. Has never been caught yet,' said Juan. 'It really is most impressive. We're delighted you've got her.'

'Are you looking for her for other things?'

'We have her on the books for at least ten other killings. Her name is Camila Diaz. She operates out of Seville. That was her home when she grew up and is still her home. She's expensive to hire, though. She's suspected of other killings, but we haven't managed to, how do you say, put the finger on her for them? We're hoping now you've trapped her, we'll be able to take fingerprints, take DNA, and place her at these scenes of crime.'

'We're delighted to help,' said Susan. 'Is there anything else you can tell me about her, though? We know that she's been hired to commit a killing here, but we don't know by who. We're trying to understand how she operates.'

'Well,' said Juan. 'It's not so easy. We have traced her, but she's very expensive, generally only used by high-end clientele. She's a top markswoman and she'll kill anyone.'

'With us,' said Susan, 'she joined a group of women who were being trafficked and hired to be used for sex. She joined in with them and then killed one man there using cyanide, but she also then looked to burn him alive. We believe it was meant to look like suicide.'

'A perfect type of killing, then. There must have been reasons to make it look like suicide though,' said Juan. 'Do you know any of these reasons?'

'Probably to make everything run smoothly in regards to the inheritance left by the deceased. We're still waiting for confirmation of that, where the money goes to. It's not been that easy to find out. There are investigations being carried out around who exactly is, or isn't, the deceased man's child. Also, his estranged wife no longer has a claim, so there's several factors to take into consideration.'

'Well, she is very expensive, Camila Diaz,' said Juan. 'She's known as the Silent One, or we say, El Ciencio. She operates out of Seville, as I said. We're not sure if she has someone fronting for her, or whether she meets clients herself. We know she's like a ghost—very, very hard to pick up once she disappears. Although she works out of Seville, we have no confirmed addresses, no confirmed locations. We just know that several meets have happened there.'

'When you say she's expensive, how much money are we talking?'

'At least a million of what you would call your pounds.'

'A million?' said Susan. 'Well, that makes sense. She killed Donal Diamond, the rock star.'

'Yes. A troubled man, if I understand rightly.'

'Well, certainly one that let fame and fortune go to the extreme. But thank you very much.'

'I'll send over the full details by email,' said Juan. 'But if you need me again, please contact me.'

Susan closed down the call and Perry moved round close to her again, sitting down on a seat.

'Why are you not standing in shot?' asked Susan.

'Well, Juan doesn't really need to know I'm there.'

'Why doesn't Juan want to know you're there?'

'Ruffled a few feathers once. They don't enjoy being told when they've got it wrong. You have a prettier face that hasn't annoyed him in the past.'

Susan burst out laughing. 'You should have rubbed it in on him,' she said.

'No, we're trying to get information. Macleod always said that information is the important bit. Don't worry about yourself or how you feel. You get over that when you get the right result.'

'He's never been as ostracised as you have in the past though.'

'You'd be surprised,' said Perry. 'Anyway, so we know she operates out of Seville. We know that she's an incredibly expensive killer, and she's known as the silent one. She's wanted for ten other killings. But somebody's got to pay for them.'

'I think we should ring the border agencies. Run some checks on the various members of the family,' said Susan. 'See who's travelled outside of the country recently.'

'Ross called earlier. You should start with Fergus. He's been out to Europe recently.'

'Where?'

'Seville. It was a Salvation Army worker that said it. We get our intel from everybody these days,' said Perry.

'Okay, we'll get on it.'

Susan made the phone call and then sat waiting while Perry went off to check on the women in their accommodation. He came back about an hour and a half later, saying that one of them, Miranda, had been out and about. Hope reckoned she'd been over to see Larry Goodlad, offering her services.

'It's not normal, is it? Maybe she's needing the money,' suggested Susan.

'No,' said Perry. 'Something's not right with that.'

'Okay, you look into that. I'm waiting to hear back from the border authorities.'

Almost on cue, the phone rang and Susan picked it up.

'I'm looking for a DC Susan Cunningham,' said the voice on the other end.

'This is Detective Constable Cunningham. Who am I speaking to?'

'This is Marjorie Watkins from the Border Agency. We're looking into travel by the various people you've put through for us. We haven't logged anyone travelling abroad except for a Fergus Finnegan.'

'Right, and where's he gone?'

'In the last two months, he's been to Spain.'

'Spain. Whereabouts in Spain?'

'He landed in Seville.'

'And he's the only one you've got that's gone anywhere.'

'Well, we also have Larry Goodlad. He travelled to several places, but far from Seville. Much further north, Norway being one of them, and Sweden. Everything seemed to be quite far north. I'll send you through all the details.'

'That'd be much appreciated.'

She closed the call and sat with a frowning face.

'What is it?' asked Perry.

'Well, we've got Fergus Finnegan going straight to Seville.'

'Ross said he'd been there.'

'Yeah, he went on a break according to the Salvation Army man. Well, a month or two ago. Seville's where she operates out of. Fergus Finnegan's gone there.'

'Anybody else go anywhere?' asked Perry.

'The only one who's been out of the country is Larry Goodlad. But he's a record producer. He was up to Norway several times.'

'Really,' said Perry. 'That's interesting.'

'But that's miles away. Norway and Spain aren't exactly very close together, are they?'

'No, they're not. If I were you, I'd check, though. See if you can look at flights out of Norway. Just in case he's done a detour.'

'But Finnegan's right there.'

'Finnegan's also broke. Larry Goodlad's not broke,' said Perry.

'No, but he's not worth a million either,'

'No, he's not. But, by the sounds of it, Fergus Finnegan can barely get himself out the door.'

'But he had every reason to be angry, though, at Donal, I mean,'

'Angry at your brother's one thing. He's your kin. To actually kill him? And he'd have to be expecting something back from it, surely. It wouldn't just be out of hatred. And again, where does he get the money from?'

'I don't know,' said Susan. 'I really don't know. What were

you saying, though, about the women?'

'Well,' started Perry, 'one of them, Miranda, was over at Larry Goodlad's. It seems strange. Basically, she was carrying on what she'd done before, except of course she was now getting the money.'

'I thought most of them were looking to be free of all this.'

'Well, the thing was, when I had them all locked up for their own safety, I couldn't let them out. But now we've got the contract killer, and we've got the four men who were trafficking them, they are free to come and go. Despite our offer of accommodation in a secure place.'

'And she what? Went round and asked for work? Touted for it?'

'That's unclear. She's not saying a lot on that front. It's difficult to know.'

'Oh, you've got that look in your eyes. What are you thinking, Perry?'

'One problem we've got is at the moment, and it's really not making sense, is Fergus Finnegan in the frame and yet, he's got no money.'

'Nobody's got any money,' said Susan. 'Not this sort of money. We need to start looking at showbiz pals. We need to look at other people outside of the immediate circle. After all, people could have organised this killing from miles away. Do you have to actually go to Seville?'

'Nobody's saying it was her,' said Perry, 'that you met. This could have been her contact. Sounds like she also knows the place. Easier to hide. Easier to poke her nose in if everything goes wrong. I don't know,' said Perry. 'I'm probably not making too much sense. It's the old thing where the brain starts ticking and the mind can't keep up.'

'You make it sound like your brain's devoid of your mind. It's like a separate entity.'

'It very much feels like it,' said Perry. And he laughed. 'Anyway, I think Hope's off speaking to Tee-Tee. She was talking about gathering the team after that. How about you and I get some lunch?'

'That's a good idea,' said Susan. 'You've been full at it. And besides, I haven't celebrated your success in capturing the woman.'

'I'd rather keep that on the quiet. I don't want to boast about capturing a contract killer. She might not like it. I'm quite ready to take the quiet plaudits,' said Perry.

Susan laughed. 'Well, I'll buy you lunch,' she said. 'Least I can do. Come on, let's get the car.'

'Two minutes,' said Perry.

'No,' she said. 'I told you; you need to give them up.'

'I know I need to give them up. But I can't give them up for me, can I? I've tried that before.'

'Why don't you give them up for me, then? Do it for your partner.'

Perry reached inside his pocket, and pulled out a large packet of cigarettes. He handed them over to Susan. 'All right then. You're on.' Susan stood looking at the packet in astonishment in her hand.

'Are you sure?' She asked.

'Well, I can't disappoint you, can I?' Susan turned and dropped the cigarettes in the bin.

'No,' said Perry. 'Take them with you. I'll be back in to get them out of there.'

Susan laughed. 'But you could just buy a packet at the shop.'

'No,' said Perry. 'You'll know. But you've got to be with me on this. You've got to make sure I stick it out.'

'Okay, game on!' she said. 'Let's get you some lunch.'

Chapter 21

Hope watched as Macleod stepped off the small stage and saw his face change from one of professionalism to one of exhaustion. He made his way down off the steps, clear of the view of the press pack located out front.

'Oh, they're clamouring now for more,' said Macleod. 'I mean, we're not that long into this investigation. Lots of them don't get solved for weeks on end, but yet, they want us to solve it immediately.'

'Nothing new in that, Seoras. You used to have to fight them off when you were investigating.'

'Yeah, but I was quick,' said Macleod. He gave a wry smile to Hope.

'That's not appreciated,' she said. 'I'm going to speak to Tee-Tee. Want to come in and sit with me?'

'Where at?' asked Macleod.

'Round their place. I thought we should have a word with the girl.'

'It's a good idea. I've got a mountain of paperwork and an online meeting about budgets,' said Macleod. 'So yes, I'll definitely come with you. Just let me text and let everybody know I won't be there.'

'You're not down here to help at all,' said Hope. 'You're here to get out of everything else up there.'

'Don't tell them,' said Macleod, grinning. But then he turned away to go back to his task, and Hope saw his face draw in tighter. Seoras was getting older, but still had a sharp mind. Now that he was higher up the chain, she wondered if he enjoyed it. Not being in amongst the chase, did he have the same energy?

She didn't know what it was like to be his age. But what she knew, from other people of a similar age, was that things just felt a little harder. And if you didn't really get behind what you wanted to do, it became a chore to do it.

She waited out in the car for him for five minutes. And then when he stepped inside the vehicle, Hope drove over to the house of Evangeline and Tee-Tee. As they arrived, Hope took in the almost palatial style. It was a beautiful property, and out here in the depths of Scotland; Hope would have loved it for herself. John would have a heck of a long drive to his car hire firm, but then again.

She stepped out of the car and looked around her. There was a large and decorative garden. *My goodness,'* she thought, *you could put up swings there. A large slide.'*

'I'm missing the secret detail about the garden that's going to blow this case apart,' said Macleod. 'Or are you just house hunting?'

'I'm just thinking forward. You could put up swings here. A big slide. Kids would have a garden to run around in.'

'I wouldn't know. We never managed.'

'Oh, I'm sorry,' said Hope. 'Insensitive of me.'

'No, it's fine. Not insensitive—it's just what's come into your mind.'

'Well, you never know. Maybe one day.'

'What?' said Macleod as she turned. Then he clocked her thoughts. 'You weren't aiming that at me, were you?'

'Well, I wouldn't mind all this just now. But the job, it's—'

'The job requires somebody else at the other end. It's always the same with kids, isn't it? From the little I know, somebody has to be there. Some people split over that. Some people bring someone in to do it.'

'Can't leave kids with a nanny,' Hope said. 'What's the point of having them, then?'

'I wouldn't know,' said Macleod. 'But what you all have to do is have somebody to look after them. And if that person will not be you, because you're running around out here, it might have to be—'

'John.'

'Maybe he would. I mean, not many men want to stay at home with the kids,' said Macleod.

'You come from a different time. It's different nowadays. People split jobs.'

'Difficult to be part time on the murder team,' said Macleod. 'That won't work. You'll have to transfer into something else, probably.'

'That'll be all right, I get my maternity leave; I get my—'

'You will get to a point where there is no maternity leave, and somebody has to stay at home and look after them. If that's going to be you, you could be the best part of a couple of years out. And, well, who knows if your job's still here or they've put somebody else in it.'

'They have to keep it for me, don't they.'

'For your maternity, yes. After that, it gets tricky.'

'Well,' said Hope. 'It's not underway yet.'

'That's a bit too much detail,' said Macleod. 'I don't need to know until you know.'

'Oh, you'll be the first to know.'

'Maybe the second,' said Macleod. 'Might be worth telling John first.'

Hope punched him in the arm. 'Come on.'

They met Evangeline at the door, who took them through to the living room where Tee-Tee was sitting down. The girl was dressed in black again and she eyed Macleod from a distance.

'She thinks you're like a rock star,' Evangeline said to him. 'Oh, we all hear about your exploits.'

'The exploits were done with this inspector alongside me,' said Macleod. 'We work as a team.' He spoke to Tee-Tee directly, but she still watched him in that almost dismissive way teenagers do.

Evangeline left, and Hope turned to Tee-Tee.

'Have you ever met your Uncle Fergus?'

'Yes,' said Tee-Tee.

'But that was quite a while ago, when you were very young. When?'

'No, no,' said Tee-Tee. 'I saw Uncle Fergus recently, not long before Dad passed.'

'Where' asked Hope.

'I went to see Uncle Fergus in Edinburgh.'

'And what did he have to say?'

'He'd been away. He'd travelled abroad,' replied Tee-Tee. She stared away as she said it.

'Right; anywhere nice?' asked Hope.

'He didn't say, so I didn't ask. Uncle Fergus can be difficult to talk to. When he's sober, he's angry. When he's not sober, he's in a more placid form of anger.'

169

'What about yourself, though? Who do you think had it in for your father?'

'Nobody like that. There were many people who needed my father. There were some of us that loved him. Mum did. We just couldn't live with him. I loved him, too.'

Hope continued with the questioning but there was very little added by Tee-Tee about the rest of the family. Evangeline and she had been here for the last several months, so they hadn't been abroad. There were no big deposits coming out of any accounts as far as the girl knew and she hadn't seen her mum talking to any strangers. Tee-Tee left the room and Evangeline came back in.

'You didn't say that Tee-Tee had visited Fergus in Edinburgh,' said Hope.

'That's right, I didn't. That's because I didn't know she had. When did she see him?'

'She said in Edinburgh.'

'She went off a few months ago to see a friend in Edinburgh. That's right. I didn't know she was off to see him.'

'Well, it appears she did.'

'Well, it makes sense,' Evangeline said. 'Tee-Tee never got the attention from Donal that she should have got. She got handouts. Crazy handouts at times. Lots of money. Donal did not know how to deal with her. How to be with her. And then half the time he was smacked up or drunk, and she didn't appreciate that.'

'So, would she be bitter towards him?'

'Oh, no; she loved him. Absolutely loved him. Wait til you see this?'

Evangeline walked away and took a photograph out of a cupboard. She passed it over to Hope, who then gave it to

Macleod. The picture was one of Tee-Tee in a wedding dress.

'This is what she wanted, ultimately. She wanted to be given away. Her father was never there. So, she's missed the attention. He was meant to be the centre of attention, the main man in her life growing up. She's missed that. She does daft things like this.'

'She gave you that, did she?' asked Hope.

'No, of course not. I found it. I reckon she must have been looking to give it to Donal. The idea of maybe getting him to think about her getting married, give her away, something like that. She sees things a bit more simply than other people. The notion that Donal and I could sit side by side. Crazy.'

'Is there anybody else she's sought after?' asked Macleod, suddenly.

'How do you mean?'

'You've said she's missing the attention of her father. Is there anybody else that could have walked in to replace him? Someone she dotes on.'

'No, I don't think so. I would notice. But I don't think so.'

Hope thanked Evangeline for her time, but as she walked through the door, Evangeline stopped her.

'I told you before I loved Donal, and that's still true. Loved him from the day I met him. I loved him even when we separated. But this reckless parenting had to stop. And because of that, I'm actually glad he's dead. I would never tell Tee-Tee that. But I am glad he's gone. Every woman he encountered, he messed up their life. He screwed it over. It's better that he doesn't do that anymore. As painful as it is for little Tee-Tee.'

Hope said nothing. And once she turned away, Evangeline again stopped her. 'It is good he's gone. For all the women. For everybody he met, whether or not in bed. He just screwed us over.'

Hope thanked her and stepped outside with Macleod. As they walked back towards the car, Macleod asked a question.

'Is all this really worth anything without the family behind it?'

'My family wouldn't be like this,' said Hope.

'How do you know? I thought you didn't know what you got.'

'It's just one of those things we say, isn't it? When we've no real idea.'

'Tell me this though,' said Macleod; 'do you believe her? One minute she's fully in love with him; the next minute, she thinks it's a good idea he's dead. Tee-Tee suddenly is going off visiting people. And wearing wedding dresses. It's not normal behaviour, is it?'

Hope stood again, looking at the garden, and Macleod walked round to the side of her. After a moment, she broke into a smile, then went back to a solid grin.

'You know what,' said Hope, 'it's all in front of us at the moment. I can feel it. I think we're close. We just need to put the pieces together. Somebody's hiding something, and it's weird, because usually everybody's hiding something. Everybody's got their dark corner. I'm not sure that's the case in this instance. I'm not sure everybody knows what's going on either. There are a few people talking assuredly, and I wonder if they know what's happening.'

'We'll get on it then. Call your team. I'll sit in with you if you want. But it's up to you.'

'You're always welcome, Seoras. But let the team do it.'

'Is Ross likely to be back for a meeting?'

'No, he's holding off at the moment, up in Edinburgh.

If there's anything else he needs to check out, it'll be on conference link.'

'Great,' said Macleod. 'My favourite.'

'You'll have to get with it,' said Hope. 'That's how we run the team nowadays.'

'I know that,' he said. 'But I just hate to see it. I miss being in the thick of it. I miss those times of pulling everybody together. Seeing the genius of your own team is something else. You'll learn to appreciate that over time.'

'Time is something we haven't got. We need to get this thing solved soon. You said that. You said the press were starting to—'

'The press are getting fed up, so the press will start their dodgier reporting. We need to get in and get out,' said Macleod. 'Show them a clean pair of heels and some convictions. So go to it,' he said. 'Time to shine.'

Chapter 22

The image of Ross appeared on a laptop screen in the Strontian makeshift office. Gathered around the table were Macleod, Hope, Perry, Jona, and Susan Cunningham. As they were waiting for Ross to finish logging in fully, Macleod was making coffee. Beside him, Perry was unimpressed.

'Not really your job to be doing that, is it?'

'Excuse me, Constable, are you telling the DCI what he can and cannot do?'

'Of course not, Sir.'

'Don't you start *sir-ing* me.'

'Well, it always used to be sir.'

'It hasn't been sir for a while. It's Seoras, okay?'

'Okay,' said Perry. 'But it'd be a lot easier to call you Seoras if you'd let me make the coffee.'

'Do you know why I'm making the coffee, Perry?' asked Macleod.

'Because you're trying not to take charge and be over the top of everything. You're trying to let Hope run the room. You're trying to give her the space.'

'No, Perry. It's because I don't think you make very good

coffee. I hate to tell you, but Ross made far better coffee.'

Susan Cunningham was sitting only a few feet away, and she burst out laughing. Perry's face showed dejection.

'You said nothing when we were worked together before. It was always—'

'How have you worked with him for so long and not got his sense of humour?'

Perry stared at her. And then he turned round to Macleod. He had a slight grin on his face. 'I told Hope that you were incredibly perceptive, that you picked up on things. How wrong was I?'

'I'm picking up on the fact that you've changed,' said Perry. 'When I used to work with you in Glasgow, you wouldn't have cracked a joke like that. You were very strait-laced. In fact, you were positively—' Perry stopped himself.

'What?' asked Macleod.

'I shouldn't really say,' said Perry.

'Of course you can say,' said Hope suddenly from across the room.

'Yeah, we all want to hear that,' said Jona.

'What do we all want to hear?' said Ross through the screen.

'Perry's just digging himself a hole,' said Susan. 'We're just going to see if he can get any further into it.'

'You were brilliant of mind and very dull socially,' said Perry.

There was a sudden silence in the room. Hope looked across from the table, wondering whether she should interject. And then she saw Macleod look up at her and turn to Perry.

'You're right. I was very dull socially. However, now I'm the life and soul of the party. So, I make the coffee as well, all right? And if you really want to know, your coffee's not as good as Ross's. But it's okay—it'll do.'

This seemed to satisfy Perry, and he walked back towards the table.

'If nobody else is making it, of course,' said Macleod.

'Sit down,' said Hope suddenly. 'Come on, we've actually got a case to crack here.'

They sat down, coffee now in hand, as Hope called them to order.

'We went to visit Tee-Tee and found out that she spoke to Fergus Finnegan not long before Donal's death. Apparently, she went to visit him in Edinburgh. She didn't tell Evangeline though, telling her instead she went off to see a friend in the capital. Evangeline says that Tee-Tee's trying to make up for having missed out on her father's love. She said that Donal was no good as a parent. She also told me she was glad Donal was dead now, even though she loved him, because he screwed up all the women he ever met, whether or not he was in bed with them.'

'There was also a photograph of Tee-Tee in a highly fashionable wedding dress,' said Macleod.

'Why?' asked Susan.

'Evangeline was holding it out to say it was how she was trying to impress her father. I wasn't convinced.'

'Not convinced of what, sir?' asked Ross.

'I'm not convinced it's a cry for attention. Why would you impress your father by being in a wedding dress? You'd bring it home. You'd show him who you were going to marry. It's not right.'

'Well, that's one way of looking at it,' said Hope. 'What else have we got?'

'Well,' said Perry. 'the focus is clearly on Fergus Finnegan with his travel plans and everything is lining up nicely. He's got a motive. He didn't get on with his brother, hates him, but he's a drunkard and he's a drug addict. Yet he's got himself over to Spain and hired a contract killer that is way out of his price league. That's the bit that doesn't work. If he had hired some hard man from round the corner to come round and stick one on Donal, I might have said "Yeah, it fits." But this killer is out of Fergus's league. Fergus Finnegan can neither afford nor can operate in the way you need to in order to hire Camila Diaz.'

'I think you're right,' said Susan. 'I agree with that.'

'It's a good point,' said Hope, 'but we know someone has hired this killer. Is it within the small group or are we looking outside of this for some other reason?'

'Well, the only person who can afford this killer is Donal,' said Ross, 'and he's the one who got killed. There's no reason for him to have himself killed.'

'But Ross, if you inherited Donal's money, you could pay. You'd be paying later, but you could pay,' said Perry. 'You might have to double it. The price might go up. And also, wasn't it meant to look like suicide?'

'That's certainly one interpretation,' said Jona, 'if that's what they were doing. Were they burning evidence? Maybe. Was the killer buying time for herself to get away by causing the blaze.'

'Is that not a bit of an overkill?' Macleod said to Jona. 'Why a fire? Kill them, get out. Why would you be bothered? If the other woman's there, kill her too.'

'Well, that's the other thing, isn't it?' said Jona. 'So, it must have been for a reason. Set a fire to try to make it look like suicide.'

'So who's in line to inherit,' said Hope. 'With no shenanigans, who's in line to inherit?'

'Well, I checked with the lawyers,' said Ross, 'and they finally came back. What they're saying is Tee-Tee has no status. We now know that she's not Donal's child. Tee-Tee would take the inheritance from Evangeline, unless Donal wrote into his will that he's giving it to Tee-Tee directly. He's never legally her guardian, and he certainly isn't her father. So, the estate goes to the next of kin. Because his wife has given up all claims, and in fact has especially been written out of the inheritance, it falls to Fergus,' said Ross. 'Everything is lining up on him.'

'Except he's not a person who can operate like this,' said Perry. 'How do you even get hold of someone like Camila Diaz? It's not easy. Be a big shot. Somebody with a bit of clout. Somebody who can operate. You can't just be some drug addict rolling up. You're not even going to get the interview, so to speak.'

'Well, I think it's laid out very clearly,' said Ross. 'I disagree with Perry on this one.'

'I think he's got a point, though,' said Hope. 'I reckon he's got a big point. So the entire estate's going over to Fergus, is it? There's nothing for Tee-Tee?'

'That's not entirely true,' said Ross. 'The business is to go over to Tee-Tee. She'll be the new sole owner.'

'What?' said Macleod. 'So, his estate is going one way, and the business is going the other.'

'The lawyers say that he's previously got a document in stating what happens with the business. It's not inherited, so to speak. He has put her in as a de facto director, but not taking overall charge of it until he passed away as they'd written it. So, she is becoming the new sole owner of his business side, which frankly is probably worth more in the long run than the estate.'

'Who knows this?' asked Macleod.

'Unsure,' said Ross. 'I've no idea.'

'So, I don't understand it,' said Hope. 'Donal dies. Estate goes to Fergus. Yeah? Business goes to Tee-Tee.'

'The two people who definitely don't know this are Tee-Tee and Evangeline said Ross. There was an instruction in the documents not to tell them. They'll know in a week when everything's kicked in.'

Hope stood up and walked over to the makeshift whiteboard. 'Imagine you're going to frame someone for the death of Donal Diamond, and say it's to be Fergus. If we run with Perry's idea that he's not capable of organising all of this, then why has he been brought into it? Well, the estate's going to go to him, so that's fine, but the business isn't. So do we have someone who doesn't know about that arrangement, and therefore looks to blame Fergus?'

'But that makes little sense,' says Susan, 'because the estate would go down to Fergus. If it doesn't go to Fergus, where does it go after that? Not Tee-Tee. You'd have to be talking purely Fergus Finnegan's son or daughter.'

'Do we even know if he has any?' asked Hope.

'Not that I'm aware of,' said Ross.

'So what? Where does it go?' reiterated Hope.

'Would it not still fall to him?' asked Susan.

'Has he committed murder to get it? Not necessarily,' said Macleod.

'I'm confused,' said Hope. 'I'm just a bit confused about why anyone is framing Fergus. Tee-Tee doesn't know she's getting the business side. She's got no idea. Evangeline doesn't know either. Evangeline's already got five million. Tee-Tee's going to inherit that one day. I mean, they're not missing anything.'

'But money demands more money, doesn't it?' said Ross. 'How many of these people who are loaded don't want more money? They always want more, don't they?'

'I don't know,' said Hope. 'Go away, everyone; keep working on it. Take the evening and let it chew over, okay? We'll come back in the morning, work out the line of attack. But for the minute, just go on your way. Have a night, not off, but relax for a bit. We've been at this solid since it started. There's no pressing need to be in tonight on it. I think we can just relax for a bit.

'We've got our killer. We've even got our people traffickers. What we need to do now is to sit back and work out our motive. I don't think anyone's going to kill again. It's just seeing where they're coming from at the moment. It's just understanding who hired that killer.'

The team left the room, except for Macleod, and as the door closed, he turned and sat on the table, looking at Hope. 'What's up?'

'Something's nagging at me, and I don't know what it is.'

'Well, I know that feeling,' he said. 'What are you going to do about it?'

'I'm going to phone John.'

'Why? Does he know?'.

'No, but I've got to phone him. Talk to him for a bit. Then I'm going to probably mosey about my hotel room or mosey about some place for dinner.'

'Why don't you mosey about for dinner with me,' said Macleod.'

'I'm not sure I want to do that anymore,' said Hope. 'Not when you've become the life and soul of the party.'

'You realise you were partly responsible for that?'

'You were a grumpy sod back then,' said Hope.

'You've changed me a lot, and I like the change. With the things we see, you've got to have a different disposition about you, or you'll get swept away by the darkness.'

'Thanks,' said Hope.

'For what?' asked Macleod.

'Not getting in the way down here. You've done your job. You've stayed on the point. I appreciate it.'

'I've had too many years of idiots from up above being a pain.'

'I'll go phone John,' she said. 'I'll meet you for dinner later. Let's see if I can get this out of my head. Whatever it is, it's bugging me.'

Chapter 23

Hope finished her phone call with John, but she wasn't happy. He was in a good enough mood; he knew better than to ask questions about the case. So, he talked about his day, letting her just chill out and think about something else. But whatever was in Hope's mind kept coming back, again and again, until suddenly, in the middle of their conversation, she blurted out, 'there was a bra on the floor.'

'What?' said John.

'There was a bra on the floor,' said Hope.

'Where?' said John. 'I've been doing the housework. I don't think there's anything lying around.'

'No, no, no,' said Hope. 'It was here. It was in the—look, sorry, I'm going to have to go. I need to go on with this.'

'Of course,' said John. 'I'll be here, just hiring cars out.'

'Sorry,' she said. But then she closed the call down quickly.

The bra was on the floor of Larry Goodlad's temporary house. She had the photograph. Maybe she should talk to Miranda about it. That was right. She should talk to Miranda. There was something bothering her about it.

Hope got in the car, texting Macleod, and said that dinner would have to wait. He texted back that he'd hang on. But

Hope was ignoring the text and simply raced to the large accommodation that the trafficked women were now living in.

It was an open house now, except for the occasional security guard. They had to keep the press out rather than a killer. She had texted Perry to meet her there and as she pulled into the car park, she could see the cigarette being smoked. She stepped out as he threw it on the floor.

'Don't tell Cunningham,' he said. 'I'm meant to be giving them up.'

'I don't care at the moment, Perry,' she said. 'I want to see Miranda.'

'Oh, her. Yeah, I mean, she's one of the happy troupe. She's actually doing all right. I mean, I don't agree with what she did with Larry Goodlad, but at the end of the day, it's up to the women, isn't it?'

'What is it, though? What was she doing with him? Did she go to him?'

'I don't know,' said Perry. 'As far as I remember, she kept telling the girls that she'd be all right because Goodlad liked her. Goodlad is a ticket out, I think.'

'Well, he certainly likes her,' said Hope. 'I saw this bra at his house when I was there. She disappeared out the back door, but she left stuff in the front. They obviously were entangled when I arrived.'

'And what? She just left her bra on the floor?'

'Yes,' said Hope.

'I'm not being funny,' said Perry, 'but it doesn't sound like her. I've been with a lot of these women at the accommodation and she's quite tidy. She's quite perceptive. She would realise and grab—'

'We can all get caught out in a steamy moment.'

'Well, of course,' said Perry, disbelievingly.

'I've got the photo of the bra,' said Hope, frustrated by Perry's disbelief.

Hope switched on her phone, pulled up the photograph, and showed it to Perry. He shook his head.

'No, you've read this wrong,' he said.

'What do you mean?'

Perry led Hope through a couple of doors into a living room where he stood and looked around. Then he pointed to the far corner.

'I mean, that's Miranda.'

Hope looked over. Miranda was an attractive-looking girl, but she was a large build of a woman. Most of the group seemed to be young and quite slender in their build, but Miranda was one of only two exceptions. Hope was dumbstruck.

'So it wasn't from her.'

'So, he lied,' Perry said.

'He did. But I don't see how this all links in. I mean, why? Why lie about Miranda? Has he got different girls on the go here? Is he playing them?'

Perry stopped for a moment. 'Look,' he said. 'Slow down. Outside.'

Hope followed Perry outside, where he seemed to stand and look off into the distance. She was going to interrupt him, but she gave him a bit of space. And suddenly, he turned round to her, hands out wide, trying to describe with him what he was about to say.

'You need to look at like this,' said Perry, 'like everyone's lying and work out what they would have said against what they have said. So, we make an assumption.'

'What's the assumption?' said Hope.

'We got that photograph of Tee-Tee in a wedding dress. Tee-Tee doesn't know that photograph's been shown to us. Her mum Evangeline thinks she's done it to show her father what a lovely girl she is and how she can be. That's an assumption. But that photograph isn't real.'

'What do you mean?' asked Hope.

'That photograph; she's taken it without the other person in it—her spouse. Why? Evangeline's put it in our head that it's a fake to show her father what she could be like. But if it's not a fake, the last thing they need is to be seen together at that point in time.'

'Not with you,' said Hope.

'If Tee-Tee actually got married, I think Larry Goodlad's in the middle of it all.'

'Go on,' said Hope.

'If he marries Tee-Tee, he inherits the business if Tee-Tee dies.'

'Yes, he does. So, he marries her. But of course, he's got to do that prior to Donal dying. Because afterwards, it looks like a grab.'

'But nobody knows about the business.'

'No, we assumed nobody knows about the business. What we do know about the business is that Evangeline and Tee-Tee don't know about it. We do not know if Larry Goodlad did or didn't. Remember, Donal and Larry were close. They're the ones we find together with all these women.'

'Not much of a newly married man,' said Hope.

'Again, think of it. We're constantly being told that Donal sets all this up. Who said that?'

'Larry Goodlad,' said Hope.

'Exactly. Miranda's coming round to see him. Yeah? Why? The women are dealing with him direct. That's because he's the guy that dealt direct in the first place,' said Perry. 'Donal didn't bring these people in. Larry Goodlad did.'

'And that's why they're not saying it, because they could still get paid. They still have something to gain by not giving away who they're working with,' said Hope. 'If it was Donal, it's all gone anyway. It's done. There's no money.'

'Exactly,' said Perry. 'They want the money, so they will not speak. Our killer wants the money because whoever's going to pay it is still there.'

'But Larry Goodlad doesn't have the money,'

'No, he doesn't. But, as Ross said, maybe you're paying double later on. Maybe this is an investment plan. Maybe he's going to inherit all the way. Ross was being watched. Why? The deed's done. Who's watching down that end? Who's got eyes on Fergus?'

'So, to recap,' said Hope. 'When they go away, who goes to see Uncle Fergus? Tee-Tee, but Tee-Tee's actually getting married. But she said she wanted to see her Uncle Fergus. So she must have done because she knew he was there and if we cross-checked we could see if she was lying. He gets sent off to him on a trip, somehow able to afford to go over to Seville. But who's down with Tee-Tee?'

'Exactly,' said Perry. 'Larry Goodlad is with Tee-Tee in Edinburgh, and he then sends Fergus off on a trip. Fergus is so smashed, and he does not know what he's doing. Larry Goodlad is able to get in previous to this because he's gone to Europe to Norway. I bet you he travelled down. He's so slick he didn't even go near Spain by air. I wonder, did he even

186

cross the border?'

'What do you mean, cross the border?' asked Hope.

'Did he sneak in? We could check it through.'

'We could do, but we haven't got the time for that.

'So then they come back,' said Hope. 'Larry Goodlad turns round and orders these women in. He's there, he's paralytic at the party, so no one thinks it's him that's done it. And he's setting it up as a suicide job.

'The only problem is, Laura wakes up. She's not meant to but she comes in and she sees the fire in progress. She legs it. What is meant to happen, and does happen, is that Larry gets up, effectively sees a killer in there, which I think was meant to be Laura, but she's gone. I think they were going to put her in there. Somehow, they were going to put somebody tied in there with him, so it would be an act, a reckless act. It would have looked like suicide, but they've had to make it up since. Our killer gets out from the job but she's still about. She was still about!' said Hope.

'Exactly,' said Perry. 'She was still about because the job wasn't over. She killed Donal. The business was coming to Tee-Tee. Fergus would get the blame for all of this because he's been set up and the money's coming to him. But it's not the big part of the money. The big part of the money is the business. It's not about inheritance. It's about what's set up in the business. And who's put him up there? Who's worked the business the whole time for Donal? Who's been part and parcel of it and probably thinks he deserves most of it?'

'But if that's the case, things are still being watched and ongoing. They'll be looking to take out Tee-Tee.'

'Exactly,' said Perry. 'Where is Tee-Tee?'

'She should be in her house, shouldn't she?' said Hope.

'Except it's, hang on a minute, early evening. She's got a regular appointment on this day. To see a counsellor. That's right. They told me that when I was at the house. She'd gone to see her dad. By the evening, she'd then gone off to see her counsellor. All the women were already there. The party had been going on. So—'

'Where is it?' asked Perry.

'Mrs Dunstan. Mrs Dunstan.'

'We need to hurry,' said Perry. Hope put a phone call through to Evangeline. The woman picked up.

'Mrs Dunstan,' said Hope. 'I need to know where she is. Where does Tee-Tee go for her counselling appointment?'

'Why, what's up?'

'Don't ask, just tell me now. It's urgent.'

The woman gave an address.

'That's the other side of Strontian. We're miles away from it,' Hope said to Perry.

'Susan and Macleod, they'll be closer.'

'Quick, you get the car. I'll ring them,' said Hope. 'Come on, Perry; we need to go.'

As they ran out and dived inside the car, Hope's heart was pounding. They knew every week Tee-Tee had a counselling session. That's why the killer was going to remain around, to make sure she got finished off, too. Because if she didn't, then they'd have to—

Hope picked up the mobile and called her team. She prayed they would get there in time. They had to get there in time.

Chapter 24

As the car raced along, Perry behind the wheel, Hope tried to place a call for the counsellor's. It took her a while to find the number, searching through the internet. The signal dropped out every now and again in the remote region they were in. When it got through, Hope heard a recorded message telling her that the counsellor was in session and she'd return her call later.

Hope rang Macleod, checking up to see if he was on his way.

'Going as quick as I can,' he said. 'But Susan's closer than me. I'll get there ahead of you, but I won't be the first there.'

'She's going to need backup. Seoras, you need to get there. You need to get there quick.'

'I get it, Hope,' he said. 'I get it.'

Hope closed the call and then placed a call in to Susan Cunningham.

'I'm almost there,' said Susan. 'I'm on my way.'

'How long til you get there?'

'About two minutes,' said Susan.

'She's in session. I can't raise her, okay? I can't raise her. You're going have to do what you need to in order to get in. There may be somebody there. There may be somebody about.

Another killer.'

'I'll see what I see. Send backup. Make sure you get back up in with me.'

Hope closed down the call and told Perry to step on it.

'I'm going as quick as I can,' he said. 'You think it's wise telling her to go in? If it's an assassin—if it's a killer, a contract killer—she will not stand a chance.'

'We've got to protect the ones in there,' said Hope. 'It's her job.'

Perry didn't say anything back, but Hope could tell he'd mixed feelings about what she was saying. She had mixed feelings herself, after all. What chance would Susan have, if indeed there was a contract killer there? She wouldn't have a hope. But then again, the killer was locked up.

* * *

Susan Cunningham turned the last corner before seeing a small estate with several buildings. She checked the sign on the entrance, looking for Mrs Durstan's practice. She clocked it, third building along, and quickly sped there. The car was parked, not neatly but simply, and Susan flung open the door, jumping out.

She ran quickly over, up to the front door, banging on it loudly. 'Anyone in? Anyone in?' There was a sign over the door saying 'closed'. But that's where they would be, wasn't it? Was she in the back? Susan decided to try to make as much noise as possible. She thumped on the windows and started shouting. No one from inside appeared. But a passing van driver halted.

'Oi!' he shouted. 'What are you doing? What's all the racket for?'

'DC Susan Cunningham. I need to get into that building. I need to talk to Mrs Dunstan.'

'You won't get her now. She's in session. She's talking to someone. I got her just beforehand. I delivered a package to her.'

'A what?' asked Susan.

'Package. A reasonable-sized one as well. I mean, it felt kind of heavy.'

'And she took it inside,' said Susan.

'Yes,' said the driver. 'Totally.'

Susan kicked on the door and banged it again. But there was nothing. No response from inside.

'You all right?' asked the driver.

'No,' said Susan. 'Take your van. Get away. Get a good distance away.'

'Why?'

'Just do as I say, please. Get far away.'

Susan jumped into her car, started the engine, and reversed it a little. She then pointed the car at the front door. She put the foot down. As the car went into gear and lurched forward, it sped up and hit the door, not at a colossal amount of speed, but enough to knock the door off its hinges.

Susan pushed open her own door once the inflatable bag that had sprung from her steering wheel, had deflated. She had been prepared for what was going to happen, and felt all right, and indeed, bounded up onto the car bonnet, jumping inside the hallway. A door was opening at the far end.

'What the blazes are you doing?' came a voice.

'DC Susan Cunningham, are you Mrs Dunstan?'

'I'm Mrs Dunstan. Who the hell are you?'

'DC Susan Cunningham, Detective Constable Susan Cunningham. You just had a package delivered, yes?'

'Yes, I did. It's in here.'

'Tee-Tee, is she in with you?'

'She is indeed.'

Susan ran in and grabbed the cardboard package. She looked around quickly, wondering what she should do.

'Open that window,' she shouted at Mrs Dunstan.

'Why?' asked the woman.

'I just told you to open the damn window! Do it!'

Mrs Dunstan seemed to be in a flap, but spurred on by the direct instruction, she opened the window.

'Now get out! Get out now! Take Tee-Tee and run!'

'Where?' said Mrs Dunstan.

'Outside, away from this room.'

Susan raced over to the window and threw the package outside. She turned to follow Dunstan, but an almighty explosion rocked the building and everywhere around.

* * *

Perry spun the car into the small car park on the industrial estate where Mrs Dunstan's practice was being held. They'd heard the explosion. In front of them, Macleod was just getting out of his car.

'Dear God,' said Hope. 'No!'

Macleod was standing, looking somewhat rocked, before racing to the front door. Someone was near the front of a car that had been rammed in. Hope recognised it as Susan's car, blocking the exit. A hand was on the bonnet. Macleod raced over.

'Got you,' he said. 'Come on, come on.' He pulled and Perry helped him.

'They're in there,' said the woman. 'I'm Mrs Dunstan. They're in there.'

She was half shouting, her ears no doubt ringing. Hope didn't wait. And half hurdled the woman up onto the car bonnet, before jumping inside the hallway. There was dust everywhere and she immediately began to cough and splutter. She looked left and right.

'Seoras, ambulance!'

'I'm on it. Just find her. Find them,' he shouted.

Hope fought her way through the dust storm that was inside. Behind her, she heard Macleod shouting again, 'Perry, get in there. I've got her; you get in there.'

'Susan,' shouted Hope. 'Susan! Tee-Tee! Tee-Tee!'

The place was a mess. As she went further along the corridor, she saw someone lying on the floor. They were coughing, but she bent down and saw the compact frame of the teenager. Tee-Tee Turner looked shaken, but she did at least look intact.

'Are you okay?' asked Hope slowly. Beside her, Perry suddenly appeared.

'I can't see anyone else,' he said.

'We need to search. We need to—Perry, take her . . . take her outside! Go!'

'What if she's injured? What if—'

'Perry, this place could come down. Just go! Get her out of here, okay, I'll look for Susan. Once you're outside, and somebody's with her, get back in here and help me.'

'Yes, boss,' said Perry. He slid his arms underneath the young teenager, picking her up easily. He dragged her out, towards the car wedged in the front door.

Hope went further into the building. To the left, there seemed to be a reasonably intact corridor, but the one to her right was barely hanging on. The right wall looked like it was about to come down, and she stealthily crept past it, worried in case it would topple on to her.

Beyond that was a room, but the ceiling had come down. Everywhere was a mess. It had crashed into a desk, the ceiling breaking, falling to the floor. You couldn't see the carpet anymore, and there was just dust. More and more dust. The wall beyond had started to cave in, and in some parts, it had actually collapsed.

'Susan, Cunningham, Detective Cunningham, where are you? Come on!'

Hope could feel the tension welling up inside her. Her body shook. Tears were fighting to burst out of her eyes, but she held them back because it wouldn't help Susan. She needed to find her. She needed to—

'Anything? Have you seen anything?' spat Perry. He was gasping. Hope briefly looked at him and saw the almost snow-like coverage on him. It was as if he'd had the worst dandruff ever, but there was no amusement in it. Hope bent down and moved part of the rubble.

'Come on, Susan,' she said. 'You've got to be here, Susan!' Perry assisted, and they began to rip things away.

Then Hope stood still, looking around. Part of her thought she should just rip everything apart but she had to be careful. Some of the rest of the wall could come down at any minute. This was not a safe place.

'Is the fire brigade on their way?' she asked Perry.

'The boss is taking care of it all. He's got it under control. He's got ambulances on the way. They're okay out there. Just focus on this.'

'I am,' said Hope.

'Let's shift stuff,' said Perry. 'I'll give you a hand.'

'Don't,' said Hope. 'Total quiet, please, Perry. Listen.'

A sudden stillness came over the room. Outside, Macleod was obviously talking to the injured parties, reassuring them. And his voice trickled in. 'Quiet!' Hope wanted to shout at him. But he was doing his job, and he needed to reassure them. She needed to listen ever so carefully. There was nothing. Absolutely nothing. And then she saw it. The slightest movement. Was that a hand? What was it?

'Perry. Over here. Over on my left. Slowly, really slowly.'

Hope looked up above her and there was a large section of brickwork ready to tumble down.

She walked across, Perry following her. Slowly, Hope lifted a piece of the ceiling. Underneath, she saw the blonde hair in the ponytail. There was no movement. Hope bent down.

'Is she?' asked Perry. Hope put her hand up. She leaned down again, listening closely. For a moment, it felt like her own heart had stopped. Then she heard the breath. It wasn't the strongest breath she'd ever heard, but it was a breath.

'Hope,' said Perry. Hope simply nodded. 'We're going to have to get her out of here, Perry. That wall's going to come down very soon. She's not conscious. I think she's unconscious, but she's breathing.'

'You lift her out,' said Perry. 'I'll hold the wall up.'

'I can't ask you to be under that wall,' said Hope. 'If that wall goes—'

'If we don't hold the wall up and you move her and it comes down, she's dead,' said Perry. 'I'm doing this. I don't give a damn. I am doing this. Get her out.'

Hope looked at the man's face. The stress that both of them were under was immense. It was a gamble. They should walk away, should wait for the fire brigade to come in. They could secure the building. Hope looked at the wall. *It may not even be up by the time they get here.*

She looked at Perry and nodded. Slowly, Hope bent down, putting both arms underneath Susan's shoulders, and she went to drag her forward. As she did so, part of the ceiling that was on top of Susan moved. It nudged into the wall and several bricks started to come down. Perry turned, pushing his back up against the wall, bracing it.

'Are you okay, Perry?'

There was no reply. Hope pulled, then realised that Susan's leg was caught on something. But how? The leg shouldn't have—Hope pulled again.

'Hold it, Perry. I need to get under here. I need to—'

'Just do it,' he said. Hope pushed up the piece of ceiling and saw that Susan's leg was not in a natural position. It was clearly broken, and broken badly. *Damn it*, thought Hope. She moved away the piece that was blocking her leg, went back to the woman's shoulders and pulled again. From all around Perry, bits of brick started to fall. 'You've got to get out, Perry. Just go. We'll risk it.'

'No,' said Perry. 'I'm not. Pull. Just damn well pull.'

Hope pulled as hard as she could. There was no point in being gentle. There was no point messing about. They had to get out of that room. Hope pulled, dragging Susan's leg. If she'd been conscious, she'd have been screaming. But Hope pulled her out into the corridor beyond, and she kept pulling as hard as she could. Beyond her, she heard a wall toppling.

'Perry!' she shouted. 'Perry!'

There was a shout from behind her. 'Get out!' shouted Macleod.

'I'm trying!' said Hope. 'I'm bloody trying!'

'Where's Perry?' he shouted.

Hope could hear Macleod jumping up onto the car. And then a pair of hands were helping her. Beyond them, they saw walls cave in. Brickwork falling. There was more dust suddenly. A plume of it. And they couldn't see back down the hall.

But they could hear it. Everything dropping. Everything feeling like a thunderous boom stabbing at their hearts.

As they reached the car, Macleod manoeuvred himself over to the other side, pulling Susan out onto the bonnet. He managed to turn her onto what, he thought, was a rough recovery position. He leaned down, listening, but Hope wasn't looking. Her eyes were back into the dust. She wanted to run down and help him. Perry was in there somewhere, but she couldn't. She couldn't see.

'Get out,' said Macleod suddenly. 'Get out, in case the whole thing comes down.' Hope stood there, looking back for Perry.

'That's an order! DETECTIVE INSPECTOR, GET OUT!'

She'd never heard so harsh a tone from Seoras. And he was right. She turned, and jumped onto the car bonnet, tears streaming down her eyes. They pulled Susan Cunningham off the car and a clear distance away before setting her back into the recovery position. The building was falling apart now. Dust was spewing out. But all Hope could do was watch that doorway.

'That's a hand, Seoras!' she shouted and raced forward.

Macleod was right on her tail. A hand hit the bonnet of the car and Hope grabbed it. Another hand came through,

Macleod grabbing it, and together they pulled. Perry was a big man, a heavy man, but Hope never felt that she had so much strength in her arms. Together they pulled him out. They heard the interior of the house collapse, the crash of masonry and brickwork, as the structure thundered down upon itself. Perry's face was a mess. There was blood all around him, but he looked up at Hope.

'She okay?' he asked.

'She's breathing,' said Hope. 'She's still breathing.'

Chapter 25

I t had taken a while to wrap everything up, although they had saved Tee-Tee and, indeed, Mrs Dunstan. There were still several loose ends. Hope had been running back up to Inverness in between and Macleod had spent most of his time back up there. The case was closed, and the press had drifted away.

They'd been there for the first couple of days, fawning over the heroic rescue. Hope had asked Macleod not to make a big deal of it, but he told her that was tough, because at the end of the day, the police needed all the good press they could get. The six-foot, red-haired detective inspector rushing to save the day was about as media ready a soundbite as there ever could be.

Hope tried to play it all down, but John was especially proud of her.

Susan Cunningham was taken to the hospital. They had worked on her leg but the weeks and months to follow would say whether it could be fixed properly. They weren't even sure if they were going to save it.

Hope went to see her, and she was slightly shell-shocked. Susan was having nightmares, waking up to loud explosions, her ears ringing, hearing nothing. She had been accompanied in the hospital by Perry during every hour he wasn't working the job. His wounds were not insubstantial, but nothing compared to Susan's. They patched him up, put several stitches in, but he never complained once. Instead, he just kept looking at Susan.

Clarissa had made an appearance. Hope requested her presence because she'd been through something like that. She'd saved a colleague. Clarissa spent some time with Perry, not to teach him how to cope with it, but just to be there as someone who understood. Hope insisted she come to the after-party, though.

They'd had to organise one near Strontian. There were so many officers and other emergency workers who had taken part in the search teams and guarding the vulnerable women. They had done a lot of the legwork organised by the local units. Jona was there with her crew as well.

Larry Goodlad had been arrested. And the long and the short of it was he would stand trial for his part in ordering the murder of Donal Diamond and the attempted murder of Tee-Tee and Mrs Dunstan.

Mrs Dunstan and Tee-Tee both made a full recovery, and the councillor was deeply grateful. Tee-Tee was rather shocked and had gone into a morose phase.

It turned out that she had married Larry Goodlad. They had gone together down to Edinburgh, and got married down there on the quiet. He'd also seen Tee-Tee's uncle, Fergus Finnegan.

Larry Goodlad had told Fergus that he had a dealer out in Seville, one who could get him plenty of gear at a reasonable price. The junkie had taken him up on it, gone out, and indeed had met somebody who had given him some gear. Then he'd returned having snorted most of it before he'd even got back to the UK.

Larry Goodlad had set it all up, even getting money for the trip to Fergus, and then had tried to kill off Tee-Tee. He'd organised the women, telling Camila Diaz when they were arriving. The woman had arrived, taken part in the debauchery that was going on. Meanwhile Diaz had killed Donal Diamond with cyanide before setting him up in what would look like a suicide attempt. But she'd been disturbed. She was going to go back and kill the girl that she'd been in bed with, because Donal had wanted two of them, not just Camila Diaz. Fortunately for Laura, she'd woken up, seen what was going on and run.

That's where the plan had gone wrong. Otherwise, Jona reckoned, the place would have burnt down, leaving not much of a trace. Certainly, trying to find out if there was any cyanide used would have been much trickier.

The package had arrived to Mrs Dunstan's, having been arranged with a courier some weeks previous—in fact, just after they killed off Donal Diamond. The second part of the plan had been carried out quietly with no obvious clues, and they almost succeeded with it.

Macleod stood beside Hope, looking at all the teams in front of them. Some dancing away to the music, others talking with their drinks. Perry was attempting to be cheered up by Clarissa.

She wasn't technically meant to be there, but that never stopped Clarissa from attending a good party. Patterson was with her, though it looked like he didn't really want to be.

'You did good, Hope,' said Macleod. 'Really good. One dead. One prevented. Couldn't have done anything about the dead one. We weren't here then.'

'You said to me a while back, 'Listen to Perry. look at where he's going with his mind. He cracked it. Saw through the lies. He saw there were possibilities. His mind is not methodical. No, it's different to that. It's like he just sees the pieces. He feels the people. It's not a description to him, it's a character. He gets that character on board inside his head. Everything seems to fit for him.'

'He does, but you went with it, and you saw some of it, too,' said Macleod.

'It cost us, though,' said Hope.

'It's not cost us yet,' said Macleod. 'She might make a full recovery, you don't know, and she'll be here. What she won't be is six feet under. You and Perry did well.'

'We didn't go by the book. I told him to get away. I told him we'd get the fire brigade in. If we had gone with that, she'd be dead.'

'But you didn't, and you got her out. Sometimes you just have to go with it. I think they call it a dynamic risk assessment.'

'Perry wasn't leaving her,' said Hope, 'and I wasn't leaving him. You told me to get out. You told me—'

'Because if you'd have gone in, you couldn't have seen him. Perry was having to get out on his own. We couldn't lose two of you in there, in that mess.'

'It was too close though,' said Hope. 'I was thinking, you said that somebody isn't all there. Ross isn't here tonight. This is the first time Ross has missed an end of the investigation party. He's never the life and soul, but he's always here. This is his duty, but he's not here. You said that somebody wasn't right, and it's Ross, isn't it? He's not taken to being a sergeant the way he thought he would, I guess. I mean, he does his job but—'

'Ross used to feel like the heartbeat of the team,' said Macleod. 'You can't be the heartbeat of the team when you've got all the responsibilities. Ross was the good guy underneath, the dependable one. As a sergeant, you've got to be selfish. Sometimes you've got to kick people into shape. Sometimes, you've got to kick the boss into shape. Ross has also got a kid at home. For the first time, he's not enjoyed himself. For the first time, he's having doubts. And I guess the kid, and the time away from the kid, is doing that.'

'I was thinking about kids,' said Hope. 'I'm not sure if I want to. That could have been me the other night. That could have been me dead. John left with a kid on his own.'

'It could have been me dead. Jane left on her own. You can't think like that, Hope. What we go through, what happens, what happened? At least if you had a kid, you wouldn't be leaving John on his own.'

'But he'd have to bring the kid up alone.'

'Or, he'd have the kid to grow up with,' smiled Macleod.

'I wasn't impressed with the way you put me in as the glamour girl. You know that.'

'I had to give the department its glamour piece. I'm sorry, but my legs don't work,' said Macleod. 'They're too white. There's hair on them. I mean, nobody wants to look at me. Well, there'd maybe be some older women.' He smiled a bit.

'People who don't look for the outside want to look at you,' said Hope.

Perry came over to the pair of them.

'How we doing, Perry?' asked Hope.

'I went up to see her today. They'll know soon enough about the leg.'

'You saved her life,' said Hope.

'I know,' he said. His hand was shaking.

'Is that nerves?' said Macleod. 'It's not like you having nerves.'

'That's a lack of fags, that is,' said Perry.

'Well, have one,' said Macleod. 'You don't have to sit in here. Go outside and have yourself a fag.' Perry shook his head.

'Why not?' asked Hope. 'You deserve it.'

Look, it's been rough starting off with us. Maybe we didn't get off on the best foot, but you know what? We came together on this one. And we did it really well. If it hadn't been for you, we wouldn't have got this, Perry. I'm seeing your strengths. Have a fag. Ross isn't even here to complain.'

'She wanted me to give them up,' said Perry.

'Who?' asked Macleod.

'Susan. She said to me, give them up. I'm giving them up. I won't have another cigarette and I'll make sure she gets better.'

'You can't determine whether or not she'll lose the leg,' said Macleod.

'No, but she can get better.'

'You did well, Perry,' said Hope. 'We're all thinking of her.'

'I'm praying for her,' said Macleod. 'You know every night on my knees.'

Perry nodded. 'It means a lot,' he said. 'I'm not a religious man like you, but the fact you take the time to do it. Thanks, Seoras, and thank you, boss.' Perry wandered off and was soon harassed by Clarissa.

'What do you think?' asked Hope.

'What do you mean?' replied Macleod..

'I've got two DCs now and I think that's something more than just a fondness for your colleague.'

'What?'

'You wait and see,' said Hope.

'Whatever,' said Macleod. 'Tonight we party and you need to be in the middle of this. If it's a karaoke, you get singing. If it's dancing, you shake your booty or whatever they call it these days.'

'And you too, you're the DCI.'

'I am the DCI, and I have to hold a level of respect up above that. I've moved on,' said Macleod.

'Are you happy with it?'

'Let's just say that retirement is looking more rosy than it did before. But I never thought I'd say that.'

'Okay, Seoras.'

'But don't worry about me,' he said. 'You did good. Taking on a lot of the traits I have. You're learning from people like Perry. One of these days, Hope, you're going to be better than me and that's all I ever wanted.'

'You'll always be better than me, so don't talk daft,' she said. 'Anyway, I suppose I better get up and dance.'

'Go save Perry,' said Macleod. 'Clarissa is trying to haul him up.'

'You go save him,' said Hope. 'You're the one she'll dance with instead of him.'

Macleod walked forward as Hope laughed. He reached forward and grabbed Clarissa's hand, pulling her out onto the dance floor.

He talked about how she'd changed, about how she was becoming the better detective, how she was learning. And there he was, learning how to be there for the entire team, even in ways that weren't him.

She hoped Cunningham would be all right.

Read on to discover the Patrick Smythe series!

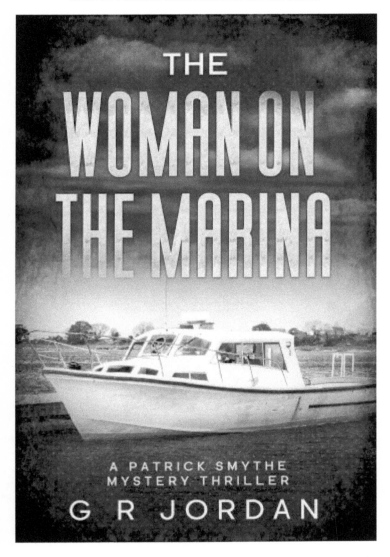

Patrick Smythe is a former Northern Irish policeman who

after suffering an amputation after a bomb blast, takes to the sea between the west coast of Scotland and his homeland to ply his trade as a private investigator. Join Paddy as he tries to work to his own ethics while knowing how to bend the rules he once enforced. Working from his beloved motorboat 'Craigantlet', Paddy decides to rescue a drug mule in this short story from the pen of G R Jordan.

Join G R Jordan's monthly newsletter about forthcoming releases and special writings for his tribe of avid readers and then receive your free Patrick Smythe short story.

Go to https://bit.ly/PatrickSmythe for your Patrick Smythe journey to start!

About the Author

GR Jordan is a self-published author who finally decided at forty that in order to have an enjoyable lifestyle, his creative beast within would have to be unleashed. His books mirror that conflict in life where acts of decency contend with self-promotion, goodness stares in horror at evil, and kindness blindsides us when we at our worst. Corrupting our world with his parade of wondrous and horrific characters, he highlights everyday tensions with fresh eyes whilst taking his methodical, intelligent mainstays on a roller-coaster ride of dilemmas, all the while suffering the banter of their provocative sidekicks.

A graduate of Loughborough University where he masqueraded as a chemical engineer but ultimately played American football, Gary had worked at changing the shape of cereal flakes and pulled a pallet truck for a living. Watching vegetables freeze at -40'C was another career highlight and he was also one of the Scottish Highlands "blind" air traffic controllers.

These days he has graduated to answering a telephone to people in trouble before telephoning other people to sort it out.

Having flirted with most places in the UK, he is now based in the Isle of Lewis in Scotland where his free time is spent between raising a young family with his wife, writing, figuring out how to work a loom and caring for a small flock of chickens. Luckily, his writing is influenced by his varied work and life experience as the chickens have not been the poetical inspiration he had hoped for!

You can connect with me on:

🌐 https://grjordan.com

📘 https://facebook.com/carpetlessleprechaun

Subscribe to my newsletter:

✉ https://bit.ly/PatrickSmythe

Also by G R Jordan

G R Jordan writes across multiple genres including crime, dark and action adventure fantasy, feel good fantasy, mystery thriller and horror fantasy. Below is a selection of his work. Whilst all books are available across online stores, signed copies are available at his personal shop.

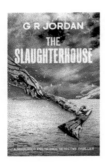

The Slaughterhouse (Highlands & Islands Detective Book 34)
https://grjordan.com/product/the-slaughterhouse
A horror movie celebrating its sixtieth year. A copycat murderer enacting the scenes from the movie. Can Macleod spot the celluloid fan amongst terrified public, or will the killer bring the curtain down on a bloody final scene?

When a gory slasher film from the sixties makes a controversial comeback, a killer takes up the lead character's mantle. Dark murderous scenes are carried out in real life, and DCI Macleod is called to lead the manhunt for the celluloid butcher. But when the final scene calls for the death of the main investigator, can Macleod find his man before his own life is taken?

Never so dark were the bright lights of stardom!

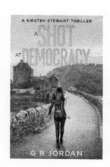

Kirsten Stewart Thrillers

https://grjordan.com/product/a-shot-at-democracy

Join Kirsten Stewart on a shadowy ride through the underbelly of the Highlands of Scotland where among the beauty and splendour of the majestic landscape lies corruption and intrigue to match any city. From murders to extortion, missing children to criminals operating above the law, the Highland former detective must learn a tougher edge to her work as she puts her own life on the line to protect those who cannot defend themselves.

Having left her beloved murder investigation team far behind, Kirsten has to battle personal tragedy and loss while adapting to a whole new way of executing her duties where your mistakes are your own. As Kirsten comes to terms with working with the new team, she often operates as the groups solo field agent, placing herself in danger and trouble to rescue those caught on the dark side of life. With action packed scenes and tense scenarios of murder and greed, the Kirsten Stewart thrillers will have you turning page after page to see your favourite Scottish lass home!

There's life after Macleod, but a whole new world of death!

Jac's Revenge (A Jack Moonshine Thriller #1)

https://grjordan.com/product/jacs-revenge

An unexpected hit makes Debbie a widow. The attention of her man's killer spawns a brutal yet classy alter ego. But how far can you play the game before it takes over your life?

All her life, Debbie Parlor lived in her man's shadow, knowing his work was never truly honest. She turned her head from news stories and rumours. But when he was disposed of for his smile to placate a rival crime lord, Jac Moonshine was born. And when Debbie is paid compensation for her loss like her car was written off, Jac decides that enough is enough.

Get on board with this tongue-in-cheek revenge thriller that will make you question how far you would go to avenge a loved one, and how much you would enjoy it!

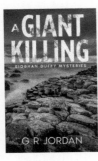

A Giant Killing (Siobhan Duffy Mysteries #1)

https://grjordan.com/product/a-giant-killing

A body lies on the Giant's boot. Discord, as the master of secrets has been found. Can former spy Siobhan Duffy find the killer before they execute her former colleagues?

When retired operative Siobhan Duffy sees the killing of her former master in the paper, her unease sends her down a path of discovery and fear. Aided by her young housekeeper and scruff of a gardener, Siobhan begins a quest to discover the reason for her spy boss' death and unravels a can of worms today's masters would rather keep closed. But in a world of secrets, the difference between revenge and simple, if brutal, housekeeping becomes the hardest truth to know.

The past is a child who never leaves home!